Which cowboy will become the first daddy in Cactus, Texas?

Their moms want grandchildren—
and these conniving matchmakers will
stop at nothing to turn their cowboy
sons into family men!
Who'll be the first to fall?

Cal Baxter
or
Spence Hauk
or
Tuck Langford
or
Mac Gibbons

4 TOTS
for 4 TEXANS

Dear Reader,

After the Randalls, I didn't think I'd find four men as lovable, or hardheaded, as those cowboys. But as I turned to my native Texas for inspiration, lo and behold, there they were. Not brothers, but best friends for life.

Cal, Spence, Tuck and Mac grew up together in a small west Texas town. Oil on their family properties could have made it easy for them, but they've worked hard all their lives. They know the value of work...and friendship. Nothing can come between them, especially women. In fact, they'd vowed long ago not to marry. Or to kiss girls, either, but Tuck dismissed that promise when he was thirteen. It didn't take the others long to agree. Their bodies hardened by a tough, outdoor life, their eyes keen, their hearts filled with loyalty and honesty, these four draw women the way pie on a hot summer day draws flies.

But their mothers, with only one chick apiece, want grandchildren. The other ladies in town have babies to cuddle. Why don't they? And they set out to do something about it.

I hope you enjoy these four guys and their fall for four special women. I certainly did. But don't you stampede to Texas looking for men like these. They may be out there, but we Texas ladies aren't looking to give them away!

Judy Christenberry

Surprise—
You're a Daddy!

JUDY CHRISTENBERRY

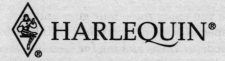

HARLEQUIN®

TORONTO • NEW YORK • LONDON
AMSTERDAM • PARIS • SYDNEY • HAMBURG
STOCKHOLM • ATHENS • TOKYO • MILAN • MADRID
PRAGUE • WARSAW • BUDAPEST • AUCKLAND

ISBN 0-373-16777-6

SURPRISE—YOU'RE A DADDY!

Look us up on-line at: http://www.romance.net

Printed in U.S.A.

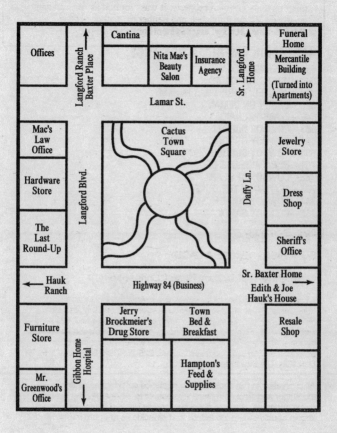

Books by Judy Christenberry

HARLEQUIN AMERICAN ROMANCE

Prologue

She was crying.

Oh, not the sobbing of some women, or the wailing of others. Not that. No, they were silent tears sliding down her silken cheeks. But tears that didn't lessen her beauty one bit.

"Melanie?"

Her shoulders jerked and she hastily wiped both cheeks with her hands, turning even more into the dark corner of the silent room.

"Are you all right?" Spencer Hauk asked, taking a step closer.

"I—I'm fine," she assured him faintly. "All the noise—I needed some peace and quiet."

There was a lot of noise upstairs. The celebration of a much anticipated union. But he knew what she wasn't saying. Her heart was broken. She was in love with Cal Baxter, his friend and the man who had married Jessica Hoya a few minutes ago.

"Mel, it's okay. I understand." He'd understood all too well. He'd been attracted to her for quite a while, but her eyes had always been turned toward Cal. Even so, Spence hadn't been able to get her out of his mind.

She turned to look at him, her blue eyes wide, her red cheeks the only color in her otherwise pale face. Then she looked away again. "I have a headache," she said firmly.

He would've laughed at her stubborn response if he hadn't feared he'd hurt her feelings. He supposed her pride had been one of the things that had drawn him to her. "Uh-huh. Well, my shoulder's available if you need to rest that achy head."

To his surprise, she took him up on his teasing offer. She leaned against him, resting her head, which fit perfectly on his shoulder. Automatically his arms settled around her, cradling her warmth against him. He couldn't count the number of times he'd hoped—dreamed—to hold her.

She felt good. Smelled good, too—like spring when everything was young, fresh. His body stirred. Hell. It'd been a while since he'd been with a lady. And Melanie had been in his thoughts, his heart, for a long time.

He didn't want to come on to her, not when she was mourning the loss of another man. He was supposed to be comforting her. But he couldn't stop himself from letting his lips caress her warm, satiny skin just below her ear.

She shuddered, a delicious trembling that stirred him even more. Pulling her tightly against him, feeling her all the way to his toes, he whispered, "It's all right, honey. Everything will be all right."

Barely shaking her head, she burrowed deeper against him. Her soft breasts pressed against his chest, and the longing to cup their fullness, to suckle them, to— Damn! If he didn't stop thinking like that he'd lose control.

His lips returned to her neck, but suddenly she turned her head, and he found her lips instead. Like lightning ripping apart a sturdy oak tree, her kiss knocked him senseless. When he came up for air, it was only to gain strength for the next onslaught of desire as he took her mouth again.

Like an addict, unable to think, he lost himself in Melanie Rule. Just like in his dreams.

And she in him.

Chapter One

Two months later

"Any sign of a baby?" Ruth Langford asked as she placed a bowl of popcorn in the center of the game table.

"No," Mabel Baxter said with a sigh. "I'm real proud of Jessica. You all know that. But I wish she'd concentrate on a family instead of her restaurant."

"She's a modern woman," Florence Gibbons said. "That's how they are."

"I'd even take a modern woman for a daughter-in-law," Edith Hauk said, her lips turned down. "Not only is there no indication Spence is looking, but he also seems depressed, sad. Even distracted."

"That sounds promising, actually," Florence commented. "Maybe the something bothering him is a woman."

"No signs of that," Edith answered.

"Tuck's the same way," Ruth added. "And he's

made several trips out of town. He won't talk to us at all about what's going on.''

"Well, so far our bet has been a bust," Florence said, frowning. "The only one not affected is Mac. He acts like women don't even exist. But at least the others, except for Cal, were happier before we started any of this."

Ruth sat at the table. "Maybe we need to work harder at it. After all, we have Cal and Jessica to prove what we're doing is good."

"She's right," Edith agreed. "Even if I don't win, I want my son married. I want him to have the prospect of children. I want—I want him to be happy."

"Me, too," both Ruth and Florence said.

"So we keep trying?" Edith said, asking for confirmation.

Even Mabel agreed, offering any help she could.

"Now, let's play cards," she added. Secretly, she felt a little superior to her friends. After all, her son had married and had the possibility of a child, even if Jess and Cal seemed predisposed to waiting.

But, then, who knew what would happen?

SPENCE SHRUGGED his sheepskin-lined leather coat a little closer to block out the bitterly cold wind that blew through Cactus, Texas.

He should go on. His friends were waiting for him at Jessica's new restaurant for the celebration. Tonight was opening night. Warm food, good friends.

So what was he doing standing here in the dark, staring at the drugstore?

The same thing he'd done for the past two months. Trying to contact Melanie Rule. But a man would have to be very dense not to get the message. She wanted nothing to do with him.

It was almost six o'clock. The damned place would be closing any minute. She should be going home. He could bump into her, casual-like, ask her if she wanted to join them.

She wouldn't, of course.

Melanie Rule was pricklier than cactus, the town's namesake.

After their…encounter at Cal and Jessica's wedding two months ago, she scarcely looked him in the eye, much less talked to him.

Every time he dropped by the drugstore, she ran in the opposite direction. Only once had he caught up with her long enough to insist she let him know if their…activity had any lasting repercussions.

Fancy words for an unexpected pregnancy, Spence thought.

Just then the lights in the pharmacy went dark, except for the safety lights that remained on all night. His throat tightened as he waited expectantly, his gaze fixed on the front door.

No one appeared.

Then he heard a car motor turn over. A minute later Jerry Brockmeier, owner of the drugstore, pulled out of the alley and drove past him.

Damn, he'd stood here freezing his tail off for nothing.

Shaking his head at his own foolishness, he turned and stomped across the town square to the newly opened The Last Roundup. He was going to enjoy himslf, damn it!

And he wasn't going to think about Melanie Rule at all.

MELANIE GREETED the latest arrivals with a smile. The new restaurant was going to be a success, she knew, just like Jessica's Mexican restaurants that she'd sold a few months ago.

At least it provided Melanie with a second job. She wanted the extra money even more now. But she wasn't going to think about that. About what had happened two months ago. About—

The restaurant door opened again, and she turned with a ready smile. And froze.

Spencer Hauk stood in the entry, staring at her.

"What are you doing here?" he demanded as if she were intruding.

"I work here," she said, turning toward the dining room. "Your friends are waiting. This way, please."

His large hand closed over her arm. "How are you?"

She swallowed, fighting to keep her smile in place. "Fine." She pulled away and led him to the large table where Jessica and Cal Baxter, the newlyweds and owners of the restaurant, waited.

Then she got the hell away from Spence.

Melanie couldn't avoid him forever. But she wanted a little more time. She wanted to stay away from his powerful presence. When she was close to Spencer Hauk, she couldn't maintain control.

Her mother had certainly told her often enough about the dangers of losing her head around men. About how her mother had forced Melanie's father to marry her so Melanie wouldn't be illegitimate. Her mother, Claudia, always paused, as if expecting Melanie's gratitude, before she continued, bitterly complaining that Melanie hadn't inspired her father to stay.

It was a litany Melanie had heard over and over again. And one she'd promised herself she wouldn't repeat. And she wouldn't.

Any baby she had would not bear that responsibility. Her baby would be loved—and wanted. Her insurance at the drugstore would help pay her medical bills. And she was putting all her salary at the restaurant into a savings account for when she couldn't work.

A loud cheer rose from the group Spence had joined, and Melanie smiled, sure they were toasting Jessica's success. Well-deserved success. Jessica had already made one fortune in the tough restaurant business. Now she was a consultant to a large conglomerate in Dallas and had the prototype for a new franchise with The Last Roundup.

Melanie didn't have Jessica's touch in restaurants,

but she had other ideas for her future. She'd been saving every penny since she moved to Cactus, determined to be her own boss someday. Now she was moving closer to her goal. The door opened again, and she resumed her duties.

"Welcome to The Last Roundup. Would you prefer smoking or non-smoking?"

SPENCE JOINED IN the celebration, happy for Cal and Jessica.

"How do you like being supported by your wife?" Tucker Langford teased his friend Cal.

Cal shot a sideways look at Jessica, who was talking to Mabel, her mother-in-law, before he answered Tuck. "It's great. I'm enjoying every minute of it," he added with a wink.

Mac Gibbons, the fourth member of their longtime friendship, nodded. "Good for you."

Tuck leaned his elbows on the table and stared at Mac. "Don't tell me you've changed your mind about marriage."

Spence waited for Mac's response. After all, he'd been the most adamantly opposed to marriage of the four of them. Maybe because he'd tried it once.

"No," Mac said slowly, as if considering his words carefully. "At least not for me. But those two were meant for each other. We've all known that for years."

Yeah, they had. Spence remembered with a smile

his friend's struggle when he'd realized he loved Jessica.

Their waitress, Nita, arrived with their steaks. She'd worked at The Old Cantina, Jessica's earlier restaurant. When Jessica began hiring here, she'd asked for a job, saying the other restaurant wasn't the same since Jessica had sold it.

After they were served and everyone was eating, Spence had his chance to question Jessica. But not about the new restaurant.

"I didn't know Melanie had quit working for Jerry."

Jessica answered. "She hasn't. She's working two jobs."

Spence frowned. "Isn't that too much? I mean—"

"A lot of people work two jobs, Spence," Mac inserted.

Tuck added, "Yeah, especially in January to pay off all those Christmas bills."

"Maybe by next year we'll have a baby to celebrate," Mabel said, her eyes sparking with happiness.

Ed Baxter sighed, then grinned at everyone. "This woman will drive us all crazy, hoping for a grandbaby." He didn't look as if he was too upset with her plans for the future.

"Mom will have to control herself," Cal said firmly. "We're not going to make decisions based on Mom's schedule. Jess needs to make this restaurant a success, to support me in my old age."

Spence laughed with everyone, since Cal was sheriff of Cactus, and his family, as the others at the table, had long ago become wealthy from oil wells. But his mind was still dwelling on another lady.

"Jess? When did Melanie ask for a job?"

Jessica looked surprised at his question. "She mentioned it at the cookout we had. Why?"

"I just wondered." That was a week or two before the wedding. Before Melanie could've possibly been pregnant. Maybe she was working two jobs because she wanted to buy something special. But he intended to find out her reason.

She hadn't said anything to him about being pregnant. Did that mean their unexpected, unplanned, er, time together hadn't produced a surprise?

He put down his silverware. "Excuse me a minute." Ignoring everyone's surprised stares, Spence strode to the front of the restaurant.

He knew he should wait. But he wasn't going to. He needed to know for sure. After all, he'd thought of little else since he'd held her in his arms. That, and hoping he could love her again—and convince her that *he* was the man for her, not Cal.

Melanie was showing a foursome to a nearby table. He folded his arms over his chest, leaned against the wall and waited.

MELANIE HANDED OUT the sparkling new menus, smiled at the customers, assuring them their waitress would be serving them soon, and headed back to her post. Automatically, her gaze scanned the restaurant, looking for any available tables. That couple looked finished. Even as she watched, the waitress delivered the check.

Consulting her list of waiting customers, she discovered the Hauks, Spence's parents, were next. Good. Their presence made her nervous. Not that they knew her. She didn't travel in their social circle.

But she felt guilty.

When she lifted her head to locate them on the benches that lined the entryway, her gaze collided with the six-foot-two hunk who had filled her dreams. What did Spence want?

Trying to ignore him, she approached his parents. "Mr. and Mrs. Hauk, your table will be ready in just a moment."

"Thank you, dear," Edith Hauk said with a smile. "I'm certainly impressed with Jess's new restaurant."

Keeping a smile in place, Melanie said, "Wait until you taste the food. And be sure and tell Jessica. They're dining in the back of the restaurant."

"We surely will. Spence, are you eating with Jess and Cal?" Edith asked, looking over Melanie's shoulder.

"Yeah," was his gruff response. "But I need to speak to Melanie a minute."

Panicking, Melanie spun around, her eyes wide. "I'm busy right now, Spence."

Much to her relief, a waitress approached to let

her know the table for two was ready. Before Spence could speak, she asked the Hauks to follow her.

Unfortunately, she didn't realize Spence had taken her literally. She turned after showing the Hauks to their table and handing them their menus to find Spence blocking her path.

"Oh! You—you surprised me. Excuse me, I have guests waiting."

"I want to talk to you."

She stared at his firm jaw, his hazel eyes unflinching, and sighed. Almost every woman in the place would want to talk to Spencer Hauk. Everyone but her.

Sinking her teeth into her bottom lip, she desperately sought a reason to dismiss him. "Spence, I need this job. And I want things to go right for Jessica. So you'll have to excuse me."

"I've excused you a hundred times in the past two months. You've been avoiding me. It's time to talk."

She didn't want to. Dear God, she didn't want to face him. But she had no choice. She'd known this day was coming. She tried again. "I have a job to do."

He stared at her, his eyes burning with determination.

"Maybe there'll be a lull in a few minutes," she suggested, hoping to put him off. She knew, with the waiting list she already had, even if no one else came in, it would be an hour before she could take a break.

"You know what I'm waiting to hear, Melanie. And I'm tired of waiting."

She knew what he was waiting to hear. He wanted to know if he was on the hook for their one…encounter. If he was going to be a father. She chewed on her bottom lip. How was she going to tell him?

She wanted to throw her arms around his strong neck, lean against that broad chest, let him share her burden. And her joy. But her mother had spent her entire life teaching Melanie that having a baby didn't mean togetherness.

It meant anger, bitterness, reproof.

She didn't want those things for her baby. She'd succumbed to Spence's charm, his manliness, once. She couldn't do so again.

"Well?" he growled, following her as she headed back to her station.

"This is an inappropriate place to discuss such— such a personal thing."

"Damn it, Melanie, I've been patient. You've avoided me like I was a skunk. I'm trying to help, here. I need to know."

"I don't—" She paused, looking at his angry expression. Just like her mother had said. Well, she wasn't going to ask her baby to bear the brunt of her mistake. She may have fallen for this man, for his gentle caresses, his tender kisses, for the passion that lit up the night. But her child would not face his anger.

She scanned her list to see who would receive the next table. After calling their name, she looked at Spence. "The answer is yes." Then she walked away.

Spencer Hauk stood like a statue, staring after Melanie, trying to comprehend what he'd suspected all along.

He was going to be a father.

He was amazed by the weakness that filled his body. He needed to sit down. Backing up to one of the benches, he sagged to the wooden seat, still staring after Melanie.

A father. He was going to be a father.

"You okay, Spence?" the man next to him asked. "You look a little green around the gills."

"I'm fine." He barely kept the news to himself. He had to talk to Melanie before he could announce such an astounding thing. But he wanted to announce it. He wanted to shout it from the housetops. He and Melanie— Melanie. He'd been attracted to her for a while, but how much did he know about her?

She'd avoided him the past two months, after their—hell, he didn't know what to call it. He'd say their loving, but something about Melanie's attitude made him wonder if that was accurate. She sure hadn't acted as though she cared anything about him the past two months.

In fact, she'd acted as if she hated him.

He frowned. That wouldn't do. The mother of his child was an important part of the picture. Even if he wasn't attracted to her, the mother of his child would be important. But Melanie meant more than that to him. He'd been tortured the past two months, longing to touch her again, to talk to her, to grow closer.

She'd held him at a distance.

He watched Melanie return to her post. Standing, he moved to her side. "We need to talk."

"I'm busy."

"Tomorrow. I'll take you to lunch."

She briefly looked at him, then turned away. "Okay." Then she called another name and escorted the next couple to their table.

As if nothing important had happened.

Chapter Two

Melanie knocked over a bottle of contact lens solution, drawing Jerry Brockmeier's attention.

"You're all thumbs today, aren't you, Melanie? Good thing that didn't break or I'd have to deduct it from your salary."

With a grimace that she hoped resembled a smile, she said, "Sorry, Jerry. I'll try to be more careful."

It wasn't the first thing she'd fouled up this morning. The closer the time got to her scheduled lunch, when Spence had promised to arrive, the more her mind kept straying.

She should have written him a letter a couple of weeks ago. But it was Christmas. Somehow that hadn't seemed right, sending him what she figured he would consider to be bad news at Christmastime.

Besides, she hadn't been all that eager to tell him. She'd enjoyed hugging her secret to herself. It had made Christmas that much more special. She and her mother had long ago given up the pretense that they were a family, but now she and her baby would form a new family. Together, she thought, a warm smile curving her lips, together they would be a family.

When the bell over the front door rang, she immediately looked up. But the man entering wasn't a customer. It was Spence and he was ten minutes early.

Though she wanted to duck down behind the rows of merchandise and pretend she wasn't here, she walked forward.

"Hello, Spence. You're early."

He seemed surprised by her greeting. After checking his watch, he caught Jerry's eye. "Hey, Jerry, mind if I steal Melanie away a little early? We're having lunch today."

Melanie grimaced. Jerry was very strict about her clocking in and out on time.

To her surprise, he smiled and waved her toward the time clock. "No problem. We're not busy today. Just come back a few minutes early."

Spence frowned and Melanie saw a protest coming. She subtly shook her head no, hoping he would get the message. "I'll get my bag," she hurriedly told him, and headed to the back of the store.

After clocking out and getting her coat and bag, she took a deep breath and joined Spence. He stood there, his hands on his hips, impatiently waiting.

To her surprise, when she reached his side, he took her hand in his. The friendly gesture was touching, but it also reminded her of his last friendly overture and the resulting complication. Determined to remain strong, she tried to tug her hand free, but he tightened his hold and pulled her behind him out of the store.

"Spence, someone might see!"

He looked at her consideringly. "And that's a problem?"

She looked away. "Not for me, but you might think so."

"Nope," he said, and started walking across the square. "Are you warm enough?"

"Yes, of course." With the sharp west Texas wind, she was bundled up to keep out the cold. She wouldn't take any chances with her baby's health.

Nothing more was said until they were seated at a table near the stone fireplace in The Last Roundup where a warm fire crackled and burned.

After they'd ordered, Melanie's nerves tightened again. She didn't know what to say.

But Spence took care of that. "I've tried to talk to you several times. Why have you been avoiding me?"

She shrugged. She hadn't felt she had any choice. Two months ago Spence had offered comfort. She'd led him to a greater commitment than he had in mind. She certainly wasn't going to embroil him even more in her problem.

"I wanted to know about the baby." The momentary pleasure she was surprised to see on his face disappeared. "Why haven't you said anything before now?"

She looked down at her plate. "I didn't want to ruin your Christmas."

"Ruin my Christmas?" He frowned, and his expression only confirmed what her mother had told her. Men weren't pleased about being trapped by a baby.

When she finally raised her gaze to his face, she found him staring at her intently.

"How long have you known?"

"Several weeks."

"Why didn't you tell me then?"

She played with her silverware so she wouldn't have to look at him. "There wasn't a good opportunity. It's not something you let drop in a normal conversation. 'The weather's cold, isn't it? Oh, and by the way, we made a baby.'"

"You know I've been trying to spend some time with you. You kept putting me off. I don't think you wanted me to know." He was shaking his head in disbelief.

He was wrong. In her dreams, she'd told him about the baby, and he'd wrapped his strong arms around her, held her safe and warm, told her how happy he was about their baby. They'd planned the baby's future, filled with love and acceptance.

A future unlike her childhood.

But those were dreams, not real life. She hadn't wanted to face real life, because then she'd have to give up her dreams.

"I apologize, but it doesn't make much difference

in the long run. It's my problem. I'll deal with it.''
She worked hard to keep her voice cool, calm, hiding
the crash of her dreams.

Frowning, he reached across to take hold of her
hand. ''What do you mean? Are you considering an
abortion?'' His voice was harsh, hard.

''No! No, I won't do that.''

''I don't want you to do that,'' he assured her, and
his hold relaxed somewhat.

She pulled her hand from his and tucked it into
her lap where he couldn't touch her. She'd made
some surprising discoveries the last time he'd
touched her. His warm skin against hers made her
weak. His strength made her want more than she
should.

Nita delivered their salads and warm, crusty bread
whose aroma filled the air. Melanie cautiously tasted
the salad, hoping she could keep everything down.
Spence sliced some bread, buttered it and handed it
to her, taking her by surprise.

''Th-thank you.''

''Have you been sick?'' he asked abruptly.

With a half laugh, she said, ''Every morning for
a month.''

''You said you'd only known for a couple of
weeks.''

She grimaced. ''I took the pregnancy test two
weeks ago, but…but I suspected the truth when I
began throwing up.''

''Have you seen Dr. Greenfield yet?''

She shook her head and said nothing.

"Why not?"

She shook her head again. How could she explain? There were so many reasons. Until she revealed her pregnancy, she could avoid anyone's anger, the town's condemnation, Spence.

"I think you should go see him this afternoon. I'll call—"

"I can't."

"Why not?" he asked again.

"I have to work."

He stared at her before saying, "I'm sure Jerry will let you have the afternoon off when he learns why."

"No! You mustn't tell him."

"Look, Melanie, there may be a little embarrassment initially, but as soon as we marry, everyone will move on to another scandal." When she didn't respond, he gave her his lopsided smile and added, "I promise."

And that's when she stopped him cold. "But we're not going to marry, Spence."

SPENCE WAS STILL STARING at Melanie, his mouth open, when Nita brought their steaks.

"Is something wrong with your salads?" she asked.

He assured her they were fine. When she offered to take the steaks back to the kitchen to keep them warm, he refused, asking her to leave them. He didn't want any more interruptions.

After Nita departed, he took a deep breath. "What do you mean, we're not going to marry?"

Melanie toyed with a piece of lettuce. "It's all right, Spence. The baby is my responsibility, not yours."

"Are you saying the baby isn't mine? That you've been with someone else?" He couldn't believe the anger that filled him, the need to know she was carrying his baby.

Already in his head he'd taken the baby into his heart, into his future. He and Melanie and their baby. He didn't want to let go of that dream.

"No!" she returned, her cheeks flaming.

"No, it's not my baby, or no, you haven't been with anyone else?" he questioned. He wanted to be sure he got this right.

"No, it's your baby, but…but I know I took advantage of your kindness. I don't expect you to—"

Spence slammed his hand down on the table. "Well, you'd damned well better expect me to take care of my child. What kind of man do you think I am?" He hadn't meant to lose his temper, but her words surprised him. He regretted it, however, when he realized she was trembling. "Eat your lunch," he ordered gruffly. "Then we'll find somewhere private to talk."

She picked up her fork, then put it down again. "I can't," she whispered.

"Honey, I'm sorry I upset you. I promise I won't yell again. Just eat a few bites. You look like a strong wind would blow you away."

He lowered his lashes but watched her as she picked up her fork again and ate a little more salad. He was angry with himself for scaring her. Normally, Melanie was a strong woman. It must be the hormones he'd heard about when a woman was pregnant.

Waving to Nita, he asked for a glass of milk. As soon as she brought it, he swapped Melanie's tea for the milk.

When she stared at him, he smiled and said, "It's better for you." Then he cut and buttered more bread for her.

As soon as she started eating her steak and potato, he excused himself and headed for the pay phone by the rest rooms.

"Marybelle, does Doc have any openings this afternoon?" he said after identifying himself.

"You're in luck, Spence. Doc just had a two o'clock cancellation. What's your problem?"

"It's not me. Well, not exactly. It's, er, it's a pregnancy." He hadn't realized it would be so difficult to tell anyone.

"Does this pregnancy have a name?" the nurse asked dryly.

"Yeah. Melanie Rule. Hold that two o'clock, okay? I'll bring her over."

When he got back to the table, Melanie had made

a little progress on her steak and half the glass of milk was gone. "Good girl," he muttered.

She looked up, surprised. "What for?"

"Drinking your milk."

"I'm not a child," she assured him indignantly. "I can take care of myself."

He smiled. "Never hurts to have a little help." He said nothing about his phone call. He knew he'd lose any ground he'd gained if he did. He wasn't sure what Melanie was thinking, but he didn't want to find out until he got some food inside her. Already her color was improving.

When he'd finished his steak and Melanie refused to eat any more, he paid the bill and, taking her arm, led her from the restaurant. She started across the town square toward the drugstore, but he tugged on her arm, halting her. "This way."

She frowned. "Where? I don't have much time. We left early, you know."

"We have to talk." That seemed pretty clear to him.

"We will…in a few days. But I have to be back on time or Jerry will fire me."

"So let him. You shouldn't be working so hard."

She stared at him. "Spence, I need my job. The insurance will take care of a lot of my medical expenses, but I can't—"

"*I*'ll take care of the medical bills. You need to rest."

She stood resolutely still, staring at the ground.

Then she looked at him, her chin up. "I appreciate the offer, but as I was saying, my insurance will pay for most of it. As long as I keep my job."

"I don't want you to keep your job."

Her blue eyes widened. "You want me to lose my job? I told you—"

"Honey, you need to rest—not work all day and night." That much seemed obvious from the shadows beneath her eyes and the weight she'd lost. And she was his responsibility, though he was careful not to say that. She seemed determined to be independent.

But *he* would take care of her.

"I can manage, Spence. I need to save money for when I can't work. I'm hoping to take a month off after the baby is born." She crossed her hands over her stomach as she spoke.

Spence's gaze followed her hands. Somehow, that gesture made the baby even more real to him.

"Thanks for lunch," she said abruptly, and turned back toward the pharmacy.

"Wait," he called as he snagged her arm. "You've got fifteen more minutes. Come sit in my truck and rest. I won't argue with you, I promise."

"That's not necessary, really," she protested.

"As a favor to me," he urged. "My truck's right here and I'll turn on the heater."

She studied him, indecision in her eyes. Finally she said, "Okay, for ten minutes."

He opened the passenger door and helped her in.

Then he hurried to his side of the truck. He started the motor and turned the heater on low. "As soon as it heats up, I'll put it on high. In the meantime, scoot over here and we'll keep each other warm."

"Oh, no! That's not a good idea!"

"Come on, honey, I'm not going to seduce you here on the square where everyone can see us," he assured her, his eyes twinkling. Not that he wouldn't want to seduce her. He'd watched her for months, as she smiled at Cal. He'd imagined making love to her, calling himself all kinds of a fool for even thinking about such a thing when he knew she was interested in Cal. But he hadn't been able to help himself.

The one time he'd made love to her had been so…so incredible, he figured he must've imagined it. He'd like to try it again to see. But not today.

She scooted a little closer, and he met her in the middle of the bench seat, wrapping his arm around her shoulders. She stiffened, but with a low chuckle, he said, "Relax, honey, while you can."

Slowly she settled against him, letting her head rest against his shoulder. As he'd suspected, she fell asleep almost immediately. He figured she was working the seven-to-four shift at the drugstore before crossing the square to Jess's restaurant for the dinner shift. She needed the rest.

The fact that she let herself trust him, even for a fifteen-minute nap, meant a lot to Spence. He had a long way to go, but he was making a little headway. He'd convince her to trust him, to let him take care of her and their baby. Then he'd only need to convince her they could build a future together. He tightened his hold around her. Yes, they could.

When it was time for her to return to the drugstore, he called Jerry on his cell phone. Keeping his voice low, he told the man Melanie needed the afternoon off because she was sick.

"Why isn't she the one calling?"

"Because she's asleep."

"I don't give sick time so my employees can nap. You wake her up and tell her to get over here at once."

"She has a doctor's appointment, Jerry," Spence retorted. He'd considered Jerry to be a pretty good old boy, but he was rapidly changing his mind.

"What for?"

"I don't think she's required to tell you that." He kept his voice low, his gaze on Melanie's sleeping face, but he wanted to get out of his truck and go punch Jerry's lights out.

"Never mind. I'll deal with Melanie in the morning," Jerry promised.

Spence didn't like the sound of that. "You'll deal with her nicely, or I'll be in to see you," he promised before disconnecting the call. He didn't care if Jerry thought he'd threatened him or not.

He wondered if he should've told Jerry what he could do with his job, but Spence was pretty sure Melanie wouldn't appreciate his interference. He suspected she was going to be angry enough about what he'd already done today.

An hour later he discovered he was right.

"WAKE UP, HONEY," a man's husky voice said, luring Melanie from her deep sleep. But she didn't want to awaken, so she burrowed deeper in his embrace. His embrace? That thought, and the realization that a man was holding her, had her eyes popping open.

"Oh!" she exclaimed as she sat up. "I'm sorry. Your arm must've gone to sleep. Thanks for the little nap. I'll just run back to the store," she said, knowing she was babbling because she was embarrassed by her behavior. She automatically looked at her watch as she started moving and came to an abrupt halt. "Two o'clock?"

"Almost," Spence said pleasantly. "You've got an appointment with Doc at two. He had a cancellation."

Melanie stared at him. "You...you let me miss work? Jerry will fire me," she wailed.

"You're taking sick leave for the rest of the day. I called him."

She wanted to slap him. He seemed to think that would take care of everything. She started scooting to the door. Maybe if she talked to Jerry, and worked the rest of the afternoon, she could—

Spence was at her door by the time she slid out and took her arm.

"Let me go. I have to go talk to Jerry," she protested.

"Melanie, if you don't see Doc now, it could be weeks before you get in. You know how busy he is."

Dr. Greenfield was the only doctor in the county, and his patient load was huge. In his mid-fifties, he was nearing retirement and everyone was worried about replacing him.

Melanie weighed her decision. She hated to admit it, but he was right. She'd put off seeing the doctor for too long. She decided to go ahead to the doctor's office since the damage was already done. But she gave the man beside her a warning. "Don't make decisions for me, Spence. I told you I'd handle things."

"Yes, ma'am," he innocently agreed, tipping his hat in her direction.

Unwilling to trust herself to speak, she turned in the direction of the doctor's office. To her surprise, Spence turned with her. "Where are you going?" she asked sharply.

"With you."

"You are not!"

"I reckon I am, honey. After all, I made the appointment."

What was wrong with the man? Didn't he have any brains?

"Spence, if you come with me, everyone will know it's your baby."

"Yeah." He took her arm again and urged her forward. "Come on or we'll be late."

He was right. And he was much too stubborn to change his mind in a few minutes. With a sigh, she accompanied him to the doctor's office.

She was quickly shown into an examination room, leaving Spence sitting in the reception area. She thought for a moment he was going to insist on accompanying her even there, but he'd sat down with a frown.

The nurse sent her a sympathetic smile, but Melanie said nothing. She was nervous and couldn't worry about Spence now.

"Change into this gown, dear, and the doctor will be here soon."

Finally alone, Melanie took a moment to compose herself before following directions. Her day had been a difficult one so far.

Faster than she would've thought, the door opened and the nurse and Dr. Greenfield came in. She followed the doctor's directions carefully, trying to relax. He said nothing except to occasionally mutter "Hmm."

When he was finished, he asked her to dress and meet him in his office. Melanie immediately began to worry. Was this standard procedure or was there something wrong with her baby? The doctor left before she could ask any questions. The nurse helped her sit up and handed her her clothes.

"Do you need any help, dear?" she asked.

"No, but...is everything all right?" Her voice trembled but she couldn't help it. Her morning sickness had left her weak.

"Doctor will explain everything in his office," the nurse said calmly before exiting the room.

She hurried into her clothes, fighting back tears. It was impossible to control her fears. All she could do was hurry.

The door to the doctor's office stood open and she could see him seated at his desk, writing on a chart. She entered, a wobbly smile on her face. But it was immediately wiped off.

"What are you doing here?" she demanded of Spence, seated in one of two chairs across from the doctor's desk.

Both men looked at her, surprise on their faces, even as they stood.

The doctor spoke first. "I understood Spence was the father."

"I am. And I have a right to know how our baby is doing," Spence added, challenging her.

"I would've told you," she assured him.

"This'll save you the trouble." He indicated the seat next to him. "Come sit down so Doc can talk to us. He wouldn't tell me anything until you got here."

His words soothed her outrage somewhat. The doctor's words were even better.

"I'll even throw this scalawag out if you want me to," he assured her with a smile.

She almost spoke, but he continued before she could. "But it only seems fair that he should hear everything since it's his baby, too."

Looking at Spence, seeing the concern in his eyes for her baby, she reluctantly nodded her approval.

"Well, now," Dr. Greenfield said with a sigh as she settled down in her chair. "We have a little problem."

Chapter Three

Melanie's heart lurched.

She hardly noticed as Spence's hand reached for hers.

"Problem?" Her voice wobbled and she stared at the doctor, pleading with him to make the problem go away.

"It's not that serious…yet," Dr. Greenwood said, a kind expression on his face.

"What is it, Doc?" Spence demanded.

"Melanie's blood pressure is elevated, she's not carrying enough weight, and she appears to be tired."

"I knew it!" Spence exclaimed, his hold on her hand tightening. "It's those damned jobs. She's working two jobs, Doc. I told her—"

"You don't have the right to tell me anything!" Melanie exclaimed, unable to bear both her fears and his lectures.

"But *I* do, young lady," the doctor inserted. "Now, Spence, you calm down or you'll be back in the waiting room. We don't want her blood pressure to go even higher.''

Melanie watched out of the corner of her eye as Spence immediately subsided into his chair, alarm on his face. It was sweet of him to be concerned for her baby. *Their* baby, she amended.

''Have I—I hurt the baby?'' she asked quietly, afraid to hear his answer.

''Not yet. And if you do what I say, you won't.''

She eased her hand from Spence's and clasped her two tightly together in her lap. Briefly closing her eyes, she took a deep breath and asked, ''What do I need to do?''

''Have you been losing your breakfast often?''

She nodded, unable to speak.

''She said for a month,'' Spence said.

''All right. I can give you something for that, but I'd prefer to try an old-fashioned remedy first. Put crackers by your bed and eat a couple before you get up each morning.''

Spence leaned toward her. ''Have you already tried that?''

She felt like an idiot, but she hadn't really thought that old wives' tale would work. ''No,'' she whispered.

The doctor accepted her answer, but she refused to look at Spence, figuring he thought she was the biggest dummy in the world.

Picking up his pen, Dr. Greenfield began writing out a prescription. ''Now, I'm giving you some vitamin tablets that will help. But you need to eat properly and get lots of rest.''

''She'll need to quit her jobs,'' Spence said, and Melanie imagined she heard satisfaction in his voice.

But he didn't understand.

''I can't. If I'm very careful, Doctor, and promise to—''

''Tell her, Doc. Tell her she has to quit.'' Spence leaned forward in his chair.

Melanie stared at the doctor. She wouldn't do anything to hurt her baby, but once she got past this morning sickness, she thought she'd be okay. She was determined to pay her own way.

Her hand curved over her stomach, protecting her child.

''Can you cut back on your hours a little?''

Such a mild reaction, compared to that of the man beside her, was reassuring. ''Yes, of course. And…and I just started the second job, so I'm sure I'll get my second wind soon.''

The doctor asked for details about her two jobs.

She explained her duties, then promised to ask Jerry if she could come in at eight instead of seven.

''That won't be enough. Tell her, Doc,'' Spence urged.

''Young lady, why are you so determined to hold down two jobs?''

Melanie looked at the doctor and then Spence. What was wrong with them? She had a child to support. Did they think she was independently wealthy?

"Dr. Greenfield, I promise to be more careful, but I have to support myself and my baby. After the baby is born, I'll cut back to one job. So I need to save a lot of money for all the expenses."

Surely he would understand, even if Spence didn't.

Wrong.

He frowned and stared at Spence. "You're not planning on marrying?"

"Yes," he said.

"No," she said.

Then they glared at each other.

"Well, now," Doc said, rubbing his chin, "I don't want to get in the middle of this argument. But even if you won't marry Spence, Melanie, he should bear some of the expense of the pregnancy."

"No!" She hadn't even realized she'd risen until Spence insisted she sit down. "I'll be careful, Doctor, I promise. I won't do anything to hurt my baby."

With a frown, the doctor slid the prescription across the desk. "I want to see you in two weeks. If there isn't some improvement, I may have to insist you eliminate at least one job, Miss Rule, for the sake of the child. But I'll give you two weeks."

"Thank you," she whispered, relief flooding her.

"Doc—" Spence protested.

She didn't look at either man so she was surprised when he cut off his plea. She didn't know why he did, but she was grateful.

"Make an appointment with my receptionist for two weeks from now, Melanie," the doctor said gently. "And remember, we're here to help you. If you have questions, or something happens, call me."

"Yes, sir, thank you." Then she brought up the one subject they hadn't touched on. "About the bill. If you'll—"

"Send it to me, Doc," Spence insisted, his voice hard.

"No, I—"

The doctor interrupted. "I think this is one argument you should give up on, my dear. I've known Spence all his life. A more stubborn man doesn't exist."

Even though she felt overwhelmed with exhaustion, she shook her head no. "I'm not a charity case, Doctor. I have good insurance and money saved. Whatever the insurance doesn't pay for, I'll take care of it."

The doctor stared first at her and then Spence. "Give the insurance details to my nurse. We'll worry about the rest later." He shoved a piece of paper across his desk. "Go home and get some rest after you get this prescription filled."

She took the paper, and suddenly she realized that Jerry was going to know about the pregnancy the moment she gave him the prescription. "Yes, sir."

She left the doctor's office with Spence on her heels. Ignoring him, she stopped at the receptionist's desk and made her appointment for the Saturday two weeks later and gave her insurance info.

Spence held her coat for her. She didn't want to

get that close to him, but she couldn't refuse his assistance.

"Thank you," she said softly.

"Come on, let's go get the prescription filled," he said, and held the door open for her.

Once they were outside, he took her arm, moving in the direction of the drugstore.

"Wait! I can do this alone, Spence. I've taken up too much of your time."

He ignored her.

"Really, you don't have to—"

He came to a halt and turned to face her. "Melanie, quit acting like you've caught a cold. You're pregnant with my child. We're going to deal with this together."

"He'll fire me."

Spence narrowed his eyes. "What did you say?"

"Jerry will fire me if I get the vitamins there. He'll know I'm pregnant. Since I have the afternoon off, would you drive me to the next town? I could—"

"He'd damn well better not."

His response startled her. He'd been pressuring her to quit her job. Now when she figured she would lose it, Spence was up in arms?

"But you said—"

"Honey, I want you to quit working, for the sake of you and the baby. But I won't let that man bully you."

With those words, he took her arm and started across the street. As Doc said, he was a stubborn man. She followed, knowing Jerry would find out soon enough anyway. But she'd hoped to keep her condition secret for a little longer. Without a car, she wasn't going to be able to get the medicine by herself. She'd considered a car to be a wasted expense since she lived so close to work and whatever else she needed. Until now.

They entered the drugstore, the hated bell ringing as they did. Jerry, ever on watch, left his position behind the drug counter and met them halfway down the aisle.

"I thought you were sick," he said, his voice stiff with outrage.

"We have a prescription that needs to be filled," Spence said, ignoring his statement. He handed it to Jerry, and Melanie watched as the pharmacist's eyes widened.

"You're pregnant!"

She answered before Spence could. "Yes, I am."

"I can't have you working here, an unwed mother. What will people think?"

Here it came. She'd already realized he would probably fire her. He was a pompous jerk.

"They'll think you're a good employer with a kind heart," Spence said softly. "And that you're smart enough to avoid a lawsuit."

"A lawsuit?" Jerry repeated.

Melanie stared at Spence, her eyes as wide as Jerry's.

"Shall I have Mac contact you?" Spence asked, just as softly as before.

"No! No, that won't be necessary," Jerry said. He looked at Melanie. "Are you coming back to work now?"

Before she could answer, Spence said, "No. She's following Doc's orders and going home to rest. As soon as her prescription is filled."

She wasn't willing to let Spence marry her, or support her, but just for one day, he could be her knight, slaying her dragons. She'd go home and nap. Then she could do her job at the restaurant tonight.

Jerry stomped down the aisle back to his place behind the drug counter. "Shall I deduct the amount from your salary?" he asked stiffly.

"No," Spence answered again. "I'll pay for it."

Jerry gave a disdainful sniff. "I guess I don't have to ask who the father is."

"That's none of your business. And I'd better not hear that you're giving her a hard time or passing on any information. Understand?" Spence put his arm around Melanie and pulled her closer to him.

Jerry quickly filled the prescription without speaking again. In no time, after Spence paid for her vitamins, they were back out in the cold.

When he started across the square again, she pulled him to a halt. "Thank you very much. For my pills and for threatening Jerry."

"No problem. I hadn't realized he was such a bully."

She briefly smiled. No, he wouldn't be anymore. Jerry would never be in a position to threaten Spence.

"Come on, let's get you home."

"It's not far. I'll be fine."

He stopped at once. "You won't even let me walk you home?" He turned her to face him. "Why not?"

She blinked at him. "It's not far."

"Why are you still trying to avoid me? You've already told me about the baby. There's no need to try to keep me away anymore."

"I don't want you to feel obligated."

SPENCE STARED AT HER, realizing the two of them weren't thinking on the same level. "I don't understand."

She shrugged her shoulders. "I've told you I'll manage. You don't need to be involved."

"Not involved?" he demanded, irritation filling him. What was wrong with her? "Do you think you got pregnant by yourself? I was raised to be responsible for my actions, Melanie Rule, and I intend to be. Whether you like it or not."

"I don't want to be a responsibility. And I don't want my baby to be one, either. We'll be just fine on our own, thank you very much."

Frustration rose in Spence. He wanted Melanie. He wanted his baby. But at every turn she kept telling him she wasn't interested in him. He was surprised at how much that thought hurt. He'd been in love before, or at least he'd thought he had, but the pain

Melanie was causing was so much more intense. His voice turned brusque to hide the hurt.

"You're not welcome. I'll provide for my child…and its mother, whether you like it or not."

She deliberately took a step away from him, tugging her hand from his. "I think I should have some say in that."

"Nope. We both lost some choices two months ago. We can't go back now."

They reached the entrance to her apartment, though it was one flight up. She tried to dismiss him when they'd reached the bottom floor. He'd have none of it.

"To the door, honey." He could be as hardheaded as the next guy. She might want to chase him away, but he wasn't going anywhere.

With a shrug, she led the way up the enclosed stairway.

He said nothing else until they reached her apartment. Then he took the keys from her hand and unlocked the door. "Thank you for everything," she said as she stepped in and turned to face him. "I'm going to take a nap now."

Though he figured she said that to make him go away, he moved forward. "Good. But I think you should invite me in."

He could tell she didn't want to. But she finally moved aside. He stepped into a small living room, meticulously clean. He wasn't much on decor, but he liked the homey feel of it, even as he recognized she had nothing expensive in the room.

Unobtrusively, he hoped, he stuck his head in the kitchen. "Do you have any milk? I'll pour you a glass."

"I can do that. I'll drink it before I go to sleep."

"I'll do it." He swung open the refrigerator door and found a carton of milk. And not much else. "No wonder you've lost weight. Can't you afford food?"

Her cheeks flamed. "Of course I can! I told you I'm not a charity case! But I eat at the restaurant after work, a-and lately I've been too tired to fix lunch. I get something at the drugstore."

"Breakfast?"

"There's not much point because it keeps coming back up."

He poured the glass of milk, noting the shelf paper, with multicolored flowers on it, she'd placed on the shelves. It gave the room a cheerful appearance.

She took the milk from him and began drinking, as if finishing it would get him out of her apartment. When she'd drained the last of it, she walked to the sink and rinsed out the glass.

"Are you going to be all right here on your own?" he asked abruptly.

"I've been here three years on my own. I'll be fine."

"But you weren't pregnant then." His voice lowered and his eyes locked with hers as he continued. "You could move in with me."

She looked away. "I—I'll be fine. I'm saving to buy my own place. Hopefully, I'll be able to have my own house before the baby's too old. That's important to me."

"That's—admirable."

"I'm very tired," she said, making her way to the door.

He would've argued with her, asked her more questions, but the circles under her eyes were more truthful than any words.

"You'll sleep?" he asked as he followed her.

This time she gave him a genuine smile. "Like the dead."

"Call me if you need anything," he urged as he opened the door.

"You've done too much already, Spence. Don't worry about me."

"No, of course not." He was lying through his teeth.

EDITH HAUK WAITED until five o'clock the next day after seeing Spencer at Jessica's restaurant. And her call had nothing to do with the bet. After all, Mabel was probably going to win since Cal and Jessica had married.

But that didn't mean Edith had given up on marrying Spence off with the same result. She didn't mind being second, or third, or even fourth, as long as it happened. And last night, there'd been something between Spence and the pretty hostess. She didn't really know Melanie Rule, but she thought she was pretty.

"Hello?" Spence growled into the phone.

"Hello, dear. Have you had a busy day?" Every day for a rancher was busy.

"Yeah. How are you, Mom? Dad okay?"

"Of course, dear." Spence was such a fine son, so attentive to their needs. "We really enjoyed our night out at Jess's new restaurant. She seems to have come up with another winner."

"Yeah."

"And she's got such a sweet girl for a hostess. I really like Melanie." She hoped she was being subtle, but Spence wasn't giving her much to go on.

"Yeah."

Something in her son's voice told her he wasn't indifferent. But his response wasn't encouraging.

"Have you known her long?"

"Mom, don't start."

"Why, Spence, what are you talking about?"

"I'm talking about this matchmaking idea you and your friends came up with. It's over and done with. Cal got married, so it's finished."

"Well, no. The contest isn't who marries first. It's about having a baby. Just because Cal beat you to the altar doesn't mean the contest is over."

"But it's not a race, Mom. And I don't have marriage plans."

"But you could. That Melanie seems very nice."

"Look, Mom, Melanie *is* nice but…she's in love with someone else."

"Oh." As badly as she wanted her son married, Edith didn't want him unhappy, tied to someone who didn't love him. She immediately dismissed the young woman from her list of potential mates. "Did I tell you I ran into Henrietta the other day? Her oldest is coming home for a visit. You remember Joan, don't you?"

"Hell, yes, I remember Joan. And I'm not interested."

"Oh," Edith said again. She didn't have any more potential mates lined up for her son. But she'd find more. She wasn't a quitter.

"Look, Mom, I'm doing fine. Just leave my social life alone, okay?"

"Why, of course, dear. I wouldn't dream of interfering." She hoped God wouldn't strike her dead at such a blatant lie. But she was only trying to help Spence for his own good. "It's time for me to start dinner, so I'll talk to you later. Unless you want to join us?"

"No, thanks, Mom. I've got plans."

AND HE DID. He was going grocery shopping for Melanie. Not that she knew. He'd admired her before, but now he was getting to know her. A more fiercely independent woman he had yet to meet.

Of course, he knew why she wouldn't marry him, even though she was carrying his baby. She was in love with Cal. He'd understood that from the first. What happened at Cal and Jessica's wedding was understandable considering Melanie's emotional state. And the attraction he'd tried to resist.

He shouldn't have taken advantage of her. And he hadn't intended to. His idea had been to offer a little comfort. What had happened had gotten totally out of hand. He still couldn't explain it. He'd thought he could control himself. After all, he knew where her interest lay. But once she moved into his arms, his interest in her exploded. He felt like a small child playing with matches that turned into a huge blaze.

But he was responsible. He would be there for Melanie whether she wanted him to or not. Besides, taking her groceries meant he'd have a legitimate excuse to check on her.

He spent half an hour in the grocery store, carefully choosing food for her. The cashier teased him when he pushed his cart to the register.

"What's the matter, Spence? Isn't Maria buying what you like these days?"

He shrugged. "I'm just picking up a few extras to help out." There was no lie in his words. He didn't say whom he was helping out. He was being discreet.

After he loaded the two sacks into his truck, he drove to Melanie's apartment and carried them upstairs. There was no response when he knocked on her door.

Worried that she might be in trouble, he pounded louder. A door across the hall opened.

"You looking for Melanie?" an elderly lady asked.

"Yes. I'm afraid she's sick and—"

"Oh, no, she went to work at the new restaurant. I saw her leave about four-thirty."

Anger surged in Spence, but he contained it as he thanked the lady for the information.

"You brought those groceries for Melanie? Want me to keep them for her until tomorrow morning? It will save you a trip back."

Since some of the items needed to be refrigerated, he reluctantly handed the sacks to the woman, except for the box of crackers. Those he clutched to his chest.

"Thanks. I appreciate the help."

"I'll give her the crackers, too."

"Uh, no. I'll give these to her."

Then he spun on his heels and ran down the stairs. He left his truck parked outside her apartment and strode across the town square to the brightly lit restaurant.

There she was, looking sexy and sweet—a rare combination—greeting Jessica's guests.

Without a thought to their audience, anger boiling in him, he reached out and grabbed her arm, snarling, "What the hell do you think you're doing?"

Chapter Four

It was Jessica Baxter who answered.

"Why, Spence, I've never seen you so riled up. Is anything wrong?" Jessica's gaze shifted between him and Melanie.

Melanie glared at him, as if daring him to say anything.

"Uh, no, I—Melanie wasn't feeling well earlier, and I thought she was going to stay home and rest."

Jessica turned to Melanie. "Are you too sick to work, Melanie? I don't want—"

Melanie smiled at Jessica. "I'm fine. Some people are worrywarts. It's best to just ignore them."

Just ignore him? Spence thought steam was going to come out of his ears.

Jessica looked at Spence again, a smile quivering on her lips. What was funny? He—

"Why don't I seat this party while you calm Spence down?" she suggested.

Melanie didn't look pleased about the suggestion, but she nodded. Then she stepped outside.

Spence spun on his heels and charged after her. She was going outside without a coat on. The woman needed a keeper. By the time he reached her side, he'd taken off his coat. Draping it over her shoulders, he spoke at once.

"I thought you were going to rest! Why are you here working?"

"I did rest, if it's any of your business. And tomorrow is Saturday. I don't work at the drugstore, so I can sleep in. And what are you doing checking on me, anyway?" She had her hands on her trim hips, his coat draped over her shoulders and arms.

"I wasn't checking on you! I bought you some groceries." He remembered what he had in his hands and shoved the box of crackers toward her. "I bought you these!"

She grabbed the box, her cheeks red, as customers passed by them. "Good heavens, Spence, you might as well send out announcements!"

He was feeling rather unappreciated when she stepped closer to him and touched his arm.

"I'm sorry. I didn't mean to sound ungrateful, but...I'd hoped to keep the baby a secret for a little while longer. Anyway, I told you today I'd be just fine."

"How can you say that? You were exhausted. And you came out without a coat on," he protested.

"Of course I was exhausted. But that's normal for the first three months."

He didn't like the idea that she knew more about having a baby than he did. "It is? Are you sure?"

"Yes, I'm sure. And you're the one standing here without a coat." She slipped the jacket from her shoulders and handed it to him.

"No, you wear it."

"Spence, I can't stay out here. I have a job to do. Thank you for the crackers."

He took back his coat, his hand covering hers briefly. "Uh, I left the rest of the groceries with your neighbor."

She'd turned to go back up the steps, but his words stopped her. "The rest of the groceries?"

"Yeah."

She glared at him again. Just when he'd gotten used to her sweet talk. "I told you I don't need you to buy me things. And groceries? Everyone will think I'm begging!"

He tried to look at his behavior from her position, and he supposed the townspeople might think— Hell, he hadn't meant to insult her. "I figured you'd need the crackers in the morning, and…and I picked up a few other things. Some more milk." She didn't look any happier. "It's good for the baby."

At that she rolled her eyes and stomped up the steps to the front door. "Goodbye, Spence."

Did she think she was throwing him out? Jessica wouldn't let her do that! He hurried after her. By the time he got back in the restaurant, she was already taking over her job from Jessica.

"You're back, Spence?" Jessica said with a smile. "If you don't have anyone to eat with, Cal will be here in a few minutes. Join him."

Since Melanie wouldn't even look at him, or give him the time of day, he accepted Jessica's invitation. "Okay, sure." He'd originally intended to fix an omelet or something at Melanie's apartment and share it with her. In fact, he'd looked forward to spending some time with her.

Just the two of them.

"Melanie, would you show Spence to our table? And tell Nita to bring him some fried zucchini to keep him happy until Cal gets here." Jessica waved to him as she headed across the restaurant to greet some customers.

With no emotion on her face, as if he were a stranger, Melanie said, "This way, Mr. Hauk," and headed toward the back of the restaurant.

He hurried after her. "Melanie, we've got to talk."

"I told you not to worry. I won't bother you," she said softly, walking even faster.

"Not bother me?" he yelled in frustration.

She stopped in her tracks and glared at him again. "Please control yourself."

"I'll control myself as soon as you agree to talk to me about—you know what. That's not an unreasonable request."

She avoided his gaze. "I'm working tomorrow from ten-thirty to three and then five to closing. You can come to my apartment at three."

He'd have to cancel his plans to play pool with the guys tomorrow afternoon.

"Unless, of course, you have other plans," she added coolly, obviously having seen his hesitation.

"No. I'll be there," he assured her. He'd think of some excuse to give the guys. She barely acknowledged his words before turning away.

He kept his gaze on her as she walked back to the front of the restaurant. From his seat, he'd be able to watch her while he ate, too. He watched her every move, while his mind thought of the plans they needed to make for the future.

Cal slid into his chair without Spence even realizing he'd arrived. "Howdy. Heard you're joining me for dinner," he said with a smile.

"Yeah. Hope you don't mind."

"You know I don't. But by tomorrow evening, you may be tired of my face, three dinners in a row."

Which reminded Spence of something he had to tell Cal. "Uh, I'll be here for dinner, but I can't make the pool game."

"Why not?"

He faced one of his boyhood friends and thought about lying. That had never happened before. "Something came up."

"Damn. When Jess and I got married, you and Tuck were worried that *I* wouldn't be able to make our Saturdays, but the two of you are the ones who are backing out."

"Tuck's not going to be there?" Spence asked in surprise. "Where's he going?"

Cal looked at him with raised eyebrows. "I don't know. All he said was what you said. Something came up."

MELANIE TRIED to remain calm, but she could feel Spence's gaze on her wherever she moved about the restaurant. And tomorrow they'd have a talk.

He wouldn't be happy. He seemed to feel that he should shoulder the responsibility for the baby. That was very sweet. And temporary. Her mother had talked about how her father had reacted, early on, to her pregnancy. It was after the baby came that her father had left.

She'd blamed Melanie's crying. She'd blamed Melanie, and told her over and over again, "If it weren't for you, your daddy would still be here and I wouldn't have to work myself to death to pay for you." Melanie heard those words still. No wonder, since her mother had repeated them until she left home. Now she only heard them when she called her. Which wasn't often.

No, Melanie wasn't going to base a marriage on an unplanned pregnancy. She was not going to be her mother.

"Melanie? You all right?" Jessica asked, and Melanie realized she'd forgotten to greet guests because she'd been dwelling on her problems.

"Yes, of course. I'm sorry." With an apologetic

smile to Jessica, she turned to the patient customers. "I'm sorry to keep you waiting. How many in your party?"

When the guests had been seated, she returned to her post to find Jessica still there.

"I didn't know you and Spence were dating," Jessica said with a smile. "I think that's terrific."

"We're not! No, we're not dating."

Jessica seemed surprised. "So he was checking on you because..." She waited for Melanie to fill in the blank.

"Because...because I was tired yesterday and he thought I was sick. So...as a friend, he thought he should."

"Oh. Well, that was thoughtful of him."

Melanie thought she looked skeptical. Fortunately, more guests came in.

This time when she came back to her post, Jessica said, "Since we're closed Monday night, I thought I'd have a little get-together to thank some people at our house. Could you come?"

Melanie liked Jessica and was pleased to be included.

But there was the transportation problem. "I'd love to, but I don't have a car and—"

"No problem. Cal can pick you up when he leaves the office. You can even meet him there at six, then you can help me when you get there early. See, there's method to my madness," Jessica assured her with a smile.

"Then, thanks, I'd love to." When Jessica strolled away, Melanie took several deep breaths. She probably should stay at home and rest. But a party sounded fun. Especially a party before the entire town knew she was pregnant.

She had a lot of plans to make before that day came.

JESSICA JOINED CAL and Spence about halfway through their dinner for a few minutes. "Is the food good?"

"You know it is, sweetheart," Cal said as soon as he finished chewing. "You wouldn't have a packed restaurant if it wasn't."

"It's great, Jess," Spence added. He got distracted as Melanie led a party of four to a table near them.

When he turned back to his companions, he discovered Jessica watching him. "Uh—"

"Oh, before I forget," she interrupted him, "I'm having a few people over Monday night and you're invited, Spence."

Before he could answer, Cal protested. "Baby, you need to rest. You know—"

"I'm fine. And I promised Melanie you'd give her a ride out to the house," Jessica said.

"I'll pick her up," Spence immediately offered.

"Thanks, Spence, but Cal's office is right here, so I'm sure he won't mind," Jessica returned.

"Sure," Cal agreed. "No problem."

Spence was disappointed, but at least he'd see

Melanie there. And maybe she'd still be speaking to him.

"We'd accept an offer to take her home, though. That way Cal won't have to go out again," Jessica said.

Spence almost swallowed his tongue to accept the offer. "Oh, yeah, sure, I'll be happy to—"

That's when he noticed Jessica's cat-that-swallowed-the-canary smile.

"I thought you would," she said softly.

"What's going on?" Cal asked.

"Nothing!" Spence snapped.

"I think something is," Jessica followed, still smiling. "I think Spence is interested in a lady."

"Melanie?" Cal asked his wife. "She seems like a nice lady. Spence, are you thinking of joining the married ranks, competing in the baby lottery?"

"No! Yes! I mean—Melanie is a friend," Spence finished, unsure what to say. He could feel his cheeks burning. But what could he say? In a few months, everyone would know about the baby. You could only hide one so long.

"Uh-huh," Cal said, staring at him.

Jessica slipped out of her chair. "Time for the band to play in the other room. Are you two going to stay for a while?"

"I'm staying until you're through, baby, and it had better not be too late," Cal warned.

"I'll hang with you for a while," Spence hurriedly added. He intended to walk Melanie home, to make sure she was safe. Hanging out with Cal would give him an excuse to be around.

"Great," Jessica said, turning to leave. Before she did so, however, she added, "Oh, by the way, Melanie gets off work at nine-thirty."

Cal stared at his wife in surprise, then turned to Spence. "Why—"

Jessica leaned over and gave him a brief kiss, stopping his question. Then she left.

"What was that about?" Cal asked. "Why'd you want to know when Melanie was free?"

Spence shrugged his shoulders. "She's been walking home by herself when she finishes here. It worries me."

"She lives in the old Mercantile building, doesn't she?" Cal asked. "She should be all right, but I'll have the deputy on duty watch out for her."

Spence didn't want someone else watching out for her. He wanted to take care of her. "I'll walk her home tonight," he said, trying to sound casual.

Cal had a look on his face that reminded Spence of Jessica's reaction, but he wasn't going to deny his interest in Melanie. Everyone would know soon enough.

They had a lot of plans to make before then.

IT WAS A BUSY NIGHT. Melanie was glad she'd bought some comfortable shoes that still looked nice. She was also grateful for the nap she'd taken. It was just a matter of adjusting. She'd be all right once she was past the first three months.

When she'd seated the last guests, she headed for the kitchen. There was a room behind the kitchen where she'd left her coat and purse.

"Say, Melanie, you want a steak before you go?" one of the waiters asked.

"No, thanks. I ate before I started work." And besides, she had a box of crackers to take home. She'd hidden them in the employees' room.

One of the chefs handed her a sealed jar. "Take some of this steak soup. It won't be so heavy, but it's got good nutrients."

"Thanks, Peter, I will." That might taste good after a brisk walk across the square in the night coldness. She retrieved her coat, tucking the crackers inside it, hoping no one would notice and ask about them. She hurried back through the kitchen, calling a good-night. When she got to the front door, however, she discovered she hadn't escaped.

"Ready to go home?" Spence stood by the door, waiting for her.

"Yes." She ducked her head and kept walking, hoping his question was casual. He held the door open for her, but his gallantry didn't stop there. He came down the steps with her.

"What are you doing?" she asked.

"Seeing you home," he said, as if his behavior was normal.

"That's not necessary. It's only a few steps."

"I need the exercise."

She dared a glimpse of his determined face, then took a deep breath. Too bad he was being so wonderful because of the baby.

"Really, Spence, I can—"

"Manage on your own. Maybe so, but I'll have nightmares if I don't know you got home all right."

She didn't know what to say, so she remained silent.

"You got the crackers?" he suddenly asked.

She pulled them out from under her coat to show him. "I really do appreciate you getting these for me. I didn't wake up in time before work, and the store is closed now." She managed a smile even as she sped along the walk.

They crossed the street and reached the door to her apartment building. She turned and extended her hand. "Thanks for coming with me. But as you can see—"

"To the door, honey, just like before."

What a stubborn man. She stared at him, but he didn't budge an inch. With a sigh, she turned and walked up the stairs, knowing Spence was behind her.

Unlocking her door, she turned to face him again. "All right, we're at the door. Thank you."

"Tomorrow, I—"

"Melanie, is that you?" her neighbor's voice called through her door.

"Yes, Mrs. Myers, I'm sorry I disturbed you."

The door across the hall opened. "Oh, no, you didn't. I was listening for you. Oh! It's you!" the lady exclaimed as she noticed Spence standing beside Melanie. "It's that nice man who brought you groceries. I thought you might want them tonight."

"Thank you, Mrs. Myers." She stepped toward her neighbor's apartment, but Spence still didn't leave.

"I'll carry them. I appreciate your taking care of them," he said to the old lady. Melanie wished he wasn't so sweet and thoughtful. It'd be easier to get rid of him.

When he emerged, escorted by Mrs. Myers, carrying two large, full grocery bags, she was appalled. "What did you buy? Everything in the store?"

He shrugged his shoulders, shifting the bags. "I thought you'd need some breakfast once you—" He broke off as Melanie glared at him. The man seemed determined to announce her pregnancy to the world.

"Mrs. Myers, why don't you take some of this food? I brought soup from the restaurant, so I don't need all of it." Particularly when she found sliced turkey, eggs, bacon, cheese, fruit, even chips and cookies. She hurriedly divided the groceries, knowing Mrs. Myers wouldn't have to shop for another week with what she was giving her.

"Oh, mercy, I can't take all that. Not when your gentleman friend wants you to—"

"Get fat," Melanie substituted with a smile.

"Don't worry about it, Mrs. Myers. I can't eat all this before it ruins. You'll be helping me out."

Spence said nothing, but he carried the food for her neighbor back into her kitchen, and Melanie heard him reassuring the sweet, elderly woman that he appreciated her helping him out.

Melanie shook her head, wondering how a good-looking bachelor, wealthy, surely spoiled, could be so sensitive to an elderly woman's pride.

The two came back out into the hall. After saying good-night and thank you again, Mrs. Myers went inside her apartment and closed the door.

Spence faced her, his expression telling her he expected a chewing out. Had she become that big a shrew? Instead she smiled at him.

"You're not mad?"

Shrugging her shoulders, she said, "You shouldn't have bought all that food. I have money for food. But—but your kindness to Mrs. Myers makes it hard to be mad at you."

"She seems nice, but she didn't have much in her kitchen, either."

"She's on a fixed income, Spence. It's not easy for her."

"There are groups in town that help."

Melanie smiled again. "There are. But she has her pride. Before I started throwing up, I'd cook enough for two and share with her every once in a while, but I'm afraid I haven't been doing any cooking. The food you gave her will help her out a lot. Thank you.''

''I did it for you,'' he said, frowning.

''I know. But I told you I can manage.'' Impulsively, she leaned forward and kissed his cheek. ''But the thought is sweet. Just don't do it again.''

His hands automatically caught her shoulders as her lips touched his skin. As she pulled away, he lowered his lips and caught hers. Their mouths clung, and he pressed her closer, longing to feel her against him. The magic he'd experienced was still there, more potent than ever.

She pulled away, her tongue sweeping her lips as he stared at her. ''We…we mustn't—there's no need to—''

''Ah, yeah, there is,'' he whispered, and kissed her again. Though the kiss was more intense, it was shorter. Melanie pulled away again.

''Spence, I told you, you don't need to be concerned. The baby and I—''

''You think that was concern? I must be losing my touch.'' Her hands were pressed against his chest, and he wanted them to circle his neck. He wanted to feel her body against his.

Instead, she took a step back, her gaze down, avoiding his. ''Thank you for walking me home and…and bringing me groceries.''

''I'll see you tomorrow.'' He knew she had no intention of inviting him in. ''Three o'clock, right?''

''It really isn't necessary.''

He took her chin between his thumb and forefinger and lifted her face to his. ''Yes, it is, honey. We've got some talking to do.'' He dropped a brief kiss on her lips, then released her to head for the stairs. ''Tomorrow.''

And tomorrow he wouldn't be satisfied with staying outside her door.

Chapter Five

Mac lined up a shot and sank the five ball in the corner pocket.

"You know," Cal said, leaning on his pool stick, "for a lawyer, you sure are a good pool player. What does that say about business? You making any money these days?"

"Damn right! I'm making money off you."

Cal chuckled. "Too bad the other two didn't make it. You'd have more of us to pluck."

"Where did you say they were?"

"Don't know about Tuck. He wouldn't say much, seemed unhappy." Cal frowned before shaking his head. "Now, Spence is another story. I think he's got woman problems."

"Woman problems? Spence? Anyone we know?"

Cal moved around the table to take his turn, since Mac had missed his last shot. "Jess says it's Melanie Rule, the pretty brunette who works at the drugstore."

Mac frowned. "I hope he knows what he's doing."

"Come on, Mac. She's a nice lady. If everyone thought like you do, the population of the world would shrink to nothing."

"No need to worry about that. Love makes fools of too many of us."

Cal thought about protesting, but he didn't want to rub his happiness with Jessica in Mac's face. He followed the cue ball to another corner of the table and took aim.

"Cal?"

He recognized that voice. "Dad? What are you doing here?"

Ed Baxter walked to the back pool table with Joe Hauk in tow. "Looking for the four of you. But I only see two."

"That's all there is today, Mr. Baxter," Mac said. "Tuck and Spence had other things to do."

"Hi, Mr. Hauk. Good to see you," Cal said. "Spence is joining us for dinner, if you're looking for him."

Joe Hauk scratched his chin. "Dinner, huh? That's only a couple of hours away. I guess I could hang around till then."

"Heck, the ladies are playing cards again tonight," Ed pointed out. "Why don't we get a little wild and have dinner with the boys?"

Joe's face lit with excitement. "Would you object, guys?"

"Not if you agree to join the game. It'll be more fun with four of us," Cal assured the older men.

"As soon as we call our wives, we'll take you on," Ed promised. "Pool is one sport where age and wisdom weigh out over muscle."

SPENCE INTENDED TO WAIT at the entrance to the old Mercantile building, but he decided he might as well go to the restaurant and walk Melanie to her door. He wondered how the crackers had worked that morning.

He stood at the bottom step to the restaurant, leaning on the post that supported the roof, his sheepskin-lined jacket fastened and his hat drawn low. It shouldn't be long now before Melanie appeared.

As he was considering their discussion, he heard footsteps running from the restaurant. Afraid something was wrong, he looked up to discover it was Melanie flying past him, going to his left, away from her apartment.

"Melanie? What the heck are you doing?" he called as he started after her. "You shouldn't be running!"

She stopped and spun around, surprise on her face.

"Did you forget our meeting?"

"Oh, yes, Spence, I'm sorry but I—I'll be there in—in half an hour, I promise."

As if she thought that would satisfy him, she turned and hurried away. He stood there, stunned.

She'd forgotten their meeting—about their *baby?* What could be more important?

He charged after her, catching up quickly and taking her arm. "Just where do you think you're going? And it can't be good for you to be sprinting all over town."

Again she seemed surprised. "Why ever not? I'm in a hurry."

"Because you're pr—"

"Don't say that! You seem determined to tell everyone. I told you I wanted to keep it secret! And turn loose of me. I have to go."

"But where?"

"To the Resale Shop," she told him, and tugged on his arm.

"Shopping? Shopping is more important than our—what we have to discuss?" He couldn't believe it. He knew women liked to shop more than men, but this was ridiculous.

"Of course not! This is business and if I don't take care of it right now, someone else might get in ahead of me." Then she took off again.

With an exasperated sigh, Spence took after her, but cowboy boots weren't made for jogs. Miss Rule was going to pay for the torture he was enduring.

He didn't touch her again, but Spence kept pace with Melanie until they'd crossed the square and gone to the second store on the business route through town. It was a dusty old shop with outdated items in the windows.

Spence knew the store. The elderly couple who ran it had lived in Cactus all their lives. He'd wondered several times lately how they managed to stay in business. It seemed to him they hadn't changed their inventory in at least a decade.

The bell over the door jingled as Melanie entered, followed by Spence.

"Mrs. Poindexter?" Melanie called.

Spence found it difficult to see in the gloomy store. Finally, he saw movement in the back and a tiny lady came toward them at a slow pace.

"Good day, Miss Rule. Have you decided on that pitcher you looked at?"

"No, Mrs. Poindexter. I came because someone at lunch today said you and your husband were thinking of closing your store."

Spence blinked in surprise. He hadn't heard that rumor, though the couple, who some said were in their eighties, was getting a little long in the tooth to run a business.

"Yes, I'm afraid so, dear. Ned doesn't like all the work the store requires, since he has a bad back."

"I wondered if you'd consider renting the space to me," Melanie asked.

Spence heard the excitement in her voice, even though she tried to remain calm. What was going on?

Mrs. Poindexter didn't answer right away. She studied Melanie, as if she were a contestant in a beauty contest. "Well, now, I don't know. It would depend on what you wanted to do here. We wouldn't tolerate any—'' her voice dropped to a whisper ''—racy kind of business, you know.''

''Oh, no, of course not. I want to do much the same kind of business as you're doing.''

Spence almost groaned out loud. What was wrong with Melanie? Couldn't she see what a disaster the store was? She wanted to sink what little money she had into something that was sure to fail?

''Uh, Melanie, you probably need to think about things before you make a decision,'' he urged.

She turned to glare at him. ''This is none of your business, Spence.''

Like a little hummingbird, quivering between flowers, Mrs. Poindexter watched both of them.

''Could I set up a time to visit with you and your husband?'' Melanie asked.

''Well, now, dear, if your husband isn't in favor of the idea—''

''He's not my husband!'' Melanie snapped.

''Oh.'' Mrs. Poindexter's gaze fixed on Spence as if questioning his presence.

''I'm a friend,'' he assured the little lady.

''I see.'' She nodded, but her gaze remained on him.

''An appointment, Mrs. Poindexter?'' Melanie prodded. ''To visit with you and your husband and discuss the possibilities?''

''Well, now, dear, I suppose we could meet Monday. It's our slow day,'' she said with a nod.

Spence looked around him at the empty store and wondered just how much slower business could get.

"Um, at four? Could we meet at four?"

"Of course we can, dear. That will be fine. But I have to tell you, this is a prime piece of property. We won't be giving it away."

"No, of course not. Thank you very much. Please don't agree to anyone else's offer until after we've talked." Melanie gave the woman a beautiful smile and almost ran over Spence as she turned to leave the store.

He'd like a smile like that one.

"Oh, sorry, Spence." She moved around him as if he were a fixture in the store, rather than there only because of her.

With a nod to Mrs. Poindexter, he hurried after Melanie. As soon as they reached the sidewalk and the door closed behind them, he grabbed her arm. "Are you out of your mind?"

She pulled from his hold and continued walking. "I don't think so."

"Melanie, that place is a disaster. They have no business. Even if anyone came in, they couldn't see to buy anything. The layers of dust on the merchandise are an inch thick."

"I know."

She kept walking.

"Where are you headed now?"

"I need to talk to Mac."

That stopped Spence. Then he hurried up again. "Mac? Why Mac?"

"You don't think I'm going to negotiate a lease without legal representation, do you? I told you I wasn't crazy."

Maybe *he* was the crazy one. She rushed in there, practically begged the woman to jack the price up on a worthless piece of property and now announced that of course she knows she needs legal help. Women!

"Mac won't be in his office."

"I'll leave a note for him to call me first thing Monday morning."

"I know where he is."

That stopped Melanie as nothing else had. "You do?"

"He's over at Lobo's playing pool." He knew that because he was supposed to be with them. Instead he was chasing a crazy woman all over town.

"Oh. I guess I shouldn't go there."

"Why not? I thought you were all determined to get this place." She'd sure seemed it to him.

"But most women don't go into Lobo's."

"I'll be with you."

She looked down at her feet, then looked up to smile sweetly. "I owe you an apology, Spence. I did forget about our meeting. I'm sorry. I just got so excited to hear about the chance to get that place, that I forgot all about it." She blushed and added,

"And I owe you for the crackers, too. I didn't get sick this morning."

He couldn't help himself. He reached out and cupped her cheek, loving its warmth. "I'm glad."

"And...and for you to be so generous to offer to take me to Mac, well, that makes me feel bad."

"Don't let it bother you." He took her hand and tucked it into his arm. "This time I get to be in the lead. It's a first for us today."

She blushed again. "I guess you think I've been running around like a chicken with its head cut off."

"Well, it wasn't that bad," he said with a laugh as they walked at a more moderate pace back to the square. "But I do think you shouldn't run around so much. It can't be good for you."

"But I have so much more energy since I kept my breakfast down this morning. If I quit throwing up, I can manage just fine. You caught me at a low moment yesterday."

"We'll see when you go back to Doc in a few weeks."

Her teeth settled into her bottom lip. "I'll be fine."

"Probably so, but I want to be sure. And we still have some decisions to make. After you get an appointment with Mac, can we still talk?"

"Yes, of course. We need to straighten a few things out," she agreed cheerfully.

But even if she did smile, Spence didn't think he liked her matter-of-fact tones.

After all, they were talking about his baby!

JOE HAUK was enjoying himself. It wasn't often that he went anywhere without his wife. He loved her dearly, but just doing things with other men was a change. Of course, he wished his son was there. Spence was his pride and joy, and he spent far too little time with him.

And today, Edith was on her bandwagon about grandkids, again.

There was a stir in the front of the pool hall and Joe looked in that direction, wondering if someone was getting ready to start a fight, not knowing Cal was in the back.

Instead, he discovered a very attractive young lady, followed by his son, passing through the front room. "Hey, it's Spence," he announced to the other three playing.

Cal looked up, then nudged Mac. "Yeah, it's Spence with Melanie."

Joe figured he'd better remember that name to report to Edith. In fact, as they came closer, he thought he recognized the young lady from the restaurant.

"Doesn't she work at Jess's restaurant?" he asked.

"Yeah, she does," Cal said. "Her name's Melanie Rule."

Joe noted that as they reached the pool table, his son slid his arm around the young lady. Yep, Edith was going to be pleased.

Spence made the introductions, though he was

clearly surprised to see his father there playing pool. It was to Mac that he then spoke.

"Mac, I know it's the weekend, but Melanie needs to make an appointment with you for Monday. Can you talk to her for a minute?"

Joe watched as Mac graciously agreed to Spence's request. The four boys, Mac, Cal, Spence and Tuck, had been friends a long time. They knew they could count on each other. Mac asked Melanie to join him in an empty booth nearby, giving his pool stick to Spence.

"All right!" Cal exclaimed. "Now we can take them, Dad. Spence isn't nearly as good as Mac."

"Hey, I spend my days chasing cows, not hanging out here," Spence protested.

"I know," Cal assured him with a grin. "That's why I know Dad and I will win."

"We'll see about that," Spence challenged, but almost immediately Joe noticed that his gaze went to Melanie.

Yep, Edith would be pleased.

ONCE SHE AND MAC had finished their business, Melanie thanked him and turned to look at Spence, who was trying to line up a shot.

"Spence, we're finished. I won't take you away from your game. But thank you for your help."

Spence put down the pool stick at once. "I'm going with you." He looked at Mac. "You're ready to take over, aren't you? I think Dad will be glad."

"Hey, now, I'm not complaining," Joe assured his son.

"You should be. I haven't been doing so well," Spence said with a smile.

"Well, maybe you were a little distracted," Joe teased.

"Really, Spence," Melanie hurried to say, "I can manage on my own, and—"

He took her arm. "I'm coming with you."

There didn't seem to be room for discussion. And, after all, she had agreed to talk to him. She said her goodbyes nicely, and headed outdoors.

Once they reached the sidewalk, she stopped again. "Do you want to go back to the restaurant?"

"No. Let's go to your place. You can put your feet up and have some milk while we work things out," he said even as he urged her in the direction of her apartment.

Once they reached her apartment, she invited him to sit down while she fixed him some coffee.

"You're not going to drink coffee, are you? Pregnant women aren't supposed to."

She sighed. The man must think she didn't care about the baby. Well, she'd straighten him out quickly enough and then he could quit worrying. "No, Spence, I'm taking care of myself. I'll drink milk." She'd given up coffee the first morning she'd gotten sick. But the smell of it didn't seem to bother her in the afternoon.

"I'll come with you," he said, ignoring the sofa and following her to the kitchen.

"Are you afraid I'll sneak a cup of coffee if you don't watch me?"

He seemed surprised by her teasing. "No. I just thought we could talk while you're making the coffee. We don't have much time and there's a lot of decisions to make."

"Decisions about what?" she asked cautiously.

"About what?" he repeated, staring at her. "About the baby. About your crazy plan to lease the Poindexters' place. About—"

She held up a hand to stop him. "Spence, I know you have some interest in the baby, but you have nothing to do with my business plans."

"*Some* interest in the baby? You make the baby sound like a movie that's come to town and will move on." He paced the length of the kitchen, which didn't take long. "Why do you think my interest will only be temporary?"

She shrugged her shoulders and turned her attention to making a pot of coffee. After she got the coffee started, she poured herself a glass of milk.

"You haven't answered my question."

She sat at the small breakfast table and took a sip of milk, trying to figure out how to explain without insulting him. "That seems to be the way most men handle an unexpected pregnancy."

"You think I'm going to lose interest in my own child?"

"Spence, babies look sweet, but they're a lot of trouble. Sometimes they cry forever and you can't figure out why. They have dirty diapers. They take up a lot of time and energy."

"So? Why does that make it only your problem?"

It was so tempting to believe his serious insistence that he wanted to be involved in his child's life, but history had taught her well.

"I don't intend to keep you away from the baby, Spence. You can come see her every once in a while. I hope you will." She smiled at him.

He stared back at her. "Come see her? Hell, Melanie, I won't have to 'come' anywhere to see the baby. 'Cause you and the baby will be living with me. That's where a wife and kid belong, with the husband and daddy."

"But—"

"Now, we need to decide when you're moving to the ranch, and when we're going to have the wedding ceremony."

She took a sip of milk to calm down. Then she got up to pour his cup of coffee as the red light went on. She set it down in front of him before resuming her seat.

Carefully wiping the moisture from her glass of milk, keeping her gaze fixed on her fingers' movement, she said softly, "But, Spence, I've already told you that's not necessary."

"I know you did. But I don't understand why. You want to explain it to me?"

She looked up at his intent gaze and swallowed. He was hard to resist, with his kindness. But she'd learned about relying on others. She took care of herself. And she paid her own way. And her baby's.

"Look, Spence, forced marriages aren't a good idea. After the first few days, a man begins to resent being forced into something. Then he gets difficult to live with, and eventually he leaves. I just don't see the point of going through all that." She tried another smile, but she didn't seem to be making much progress.

"That's because you don't understand, Melanie. I know our marriage will be different from Cal's and—I mean, other marriages. But we respect each other, and we'll have our baby to love."

"Spence—"

"I know how you feel. And it's okay. But I've wanted you for a long time. That's not going to change."

"You...you want me?"

Spence backtracked at once, fearing her rejection. "What we had was good, wasn't it? It still is. When I kiss you, I feel things— Anyway, everything will work out."

"I'm not sure—" she began.

He interrupted. He offered his best counterpoint to her argument against their marriage. Except, of course, for the argument that Cal was already married. He stared at her. "And last but not least, I won't leave."

Chapter Six

She wanted to believe him. She really did.

With a sigh, she said, "I know you think you won't leave, Spence, but...but just because we had good sex once isn't enough reason to believe things will work out. Lots of people have good sex and still get divorced."

"We won't. The baby is as much my responsibility as it is yours. Why shouldn't I want to be there as much as you?"

She shrugged her shoulders. "That's the way nature made it. We're the mothers."

"I'm not buying that. Tell me why you think I'll leave. Cactus is my home."

"Maybe you'll send me away. I like it here in Cactus. If I take care of my baby, I can stay here. If I ask you to take care of me and my baby, you can decide—"

"But I won't."

With a sigh, she realized she was going to have to

trot out her family history so he'd understand. "Spence, I've been through this before."

"You've been pregnant before?"

"No! Of course not. But my mother got pregnant when she wasn't married. My father married her but...but he was unhappy. Then he left. My mother told me, from the time I was old enough to understand, that it was my fault my daddy didn't stay. My fault she had to work so hard to support us. My fault she was unhappy."

"But that's not—"

"I know. But I've seen it with other men. I've had friends who were abandoned. It just doesn't seem smart to base a marriage on a baby."

"You think it's better for a kid to not have a daddy? For him to wonder all his life why his daddy's not there?" He paused, then asked, "Did you ever hear from your daddy?"

She shook her head, trying to look as if it didn't matter. "No, my mother heard he'd died in a car wreck when I was eight." With a wry smile, she added, "She blamed me for that, too."

"Your mother—"

"Wasn't much of a mother. I know. And I promise you I won't do that to our child. I already love her."

"Her?"

"I think of the baby as a girl."

"So you don't know yet that it's a girl?"

"No."

"Then I'm thinking it's a boy. Hauks have boys."

She smiled. He sounded as if he thought he could change the sex of the baby with positive thinking. "Girl or boy, I promise I'll take good care of the baby. And you can visit whenever you wish."

"And you think I'm the kind of guy who would settle for being a weekend dad?"

Truth to tell, nothing he'd ever done had made her think that. Spence wasn't like most men, she knew. But she didn't believe a marriage for the sake of a child had a chance of making it. Spence didn't love her. At least he hadn't said he did—not when they'd made love at the church, or since. He'd tried to contact her, true, but that was because he was responsible.

And he'd said he liked the sex. Big surprise. He was a man, after all.

"No, of course not. I'm trying to tell you that you don't *have* to marry me because I'm pregnant. I'll even let you help pay Doc's bill, if you want." A sop to his sense of responsibility might help.

It didn't work.

"That's not enough. I want to live with my child, to be there for him…for his mother. We'll—"

"I'm really tired," she said, interrupting him. "Maybe we could discuss this another time." If she listened to him much longer, she might forget reality. She stood up, hoping he'd leave her in peace.

He stood with her. "I know you need to rest. But we haven't finished discussing this, Melanie. I won't take no for an answer."

She smiled and said nothing. He couldn't argue with a smile.

He walked to the door and she followed. Opening it, he turned around.

She held her breath, afraid he was going to continue the argument. He didn't. Instead, he pulled her against him and lowered his lips to hers. The magic of his kiss held true, and she almost forgot she wasn't going to give in to him.

He released her lips and bowed his forehead to hers. ''This is getting to be a habit.''

''One that we shouldn't indulge in,'' she said softly, but she didn't move away. His warmth felt too good against hers.

''You keep saying no, but your body is saying something else.'' His lips descended on hers again, and her arms slid around his neck. This kiss reminded her of their lovemaking, taking her to those magical depths where nothing mattered but the man holding her.

''Think about it, honey,'' he whispered as he released his hold on her. Then he turned and closed the door behind him.

She leaned against it and sighed. She'd think about it, all right.

She'd think about the lesson she'd learned that evening in the church. That Spence Hauk's touch was different from any other man's.

She'd thought she was in love with Cal, but Spence had erased Cal from her mind.

She'd been aware of Spence last fall. He'd been fun, relaxed, handsome.

But she'd already fixed on Cal...because he was safe. He wouldn't leave like her father. She felt sure of that. After all, he was a lawman.

Once Spence had made love to her, she couldn't stop thinking about him, longing for his touch. She called herself a weak woman, thinking she loved one man and wanted another. But the next time she'd seen Cal, she hadn't felt any interest in him. Which was a relief since he was Jessica's husband.

That's when she realized she had a crush on Cal. Not because she was attracted to him, but because she thought he was safe.

Spence was safe, too. He wouldn't leave. But he could break her heart. And that was exactly what made him dangerous.

SPENCE WENT BACK to Lobo's. After all, it'd be at least an hour before the guys went to the restaurant for dinner. Where Melanie would already be at work.

His friends greeted him, and his father offered to let him take his place in the pool game. "No, thanks, Dad. I think I'll watch. I've got some things on my mind."

"Did you see that pretty little lady home?"

"Yeah."

When he didn't add anything else, the game went on. He watched Cal make a shot. He was a good friend. It wasn't his fault the woman Spence loved was in love with him. He had Jessica.

But Spence had his pride. He wasn't going to tell Melanie he loved her. He didn't want to hear her rejection. He figured he'd marry her and gradually let her know he cared about her. The baby was enough reason for them to get started.

Only Melanie didn't think the same way. Crazy woman.

She intended to pay her own way, to take care of the baby by herself. She didn't want any help from him. He could *visit* if he wanted.

Damn it! That wasn't right.

"You okay?" Cal asked, standing beside him.

"Huh? Yeah, sure. Just thinking."

Cal moved back to the table to play, and Spence tried to concentrate on the game. But all he could see was Melanie sitting across from him in her little kitchen.

When the game finally ended, everyone walked over to the restaurant. Melanie greeted all of them with a smile. Spence thought her smile for Cal was warmer than the one she gave him. In fact, the smile he—the father of her baby—got wasn't much of a smile at all.

"Did you get any rest?"

"Yes, thank you, Spence. This way, please," she said brightly to all of them, as if they didn't know which table they'd be using.

After they all sat, Melanie passed around the

menus. When she handed Spence his, he wrapped his hand over hers. She jerked her hand back and hurried away from the table, her cheeks red.

"Pretty lady," Joe said, watching his son.

"Yeah."

JOE HAUK WAS PLEASED. He'd been under strict instructions from his wife to pressure Spence about marrying. Now it looked as if he wouldn't have to interfere in his son's life, and that pleased him. If he was any judge of character, Spence was already in love. The boy couldn't keep his eyes off Melanie Rule.

Edith would be pleased.

And it wasn't just that damn bet. Edith really did want Spence's happiness. Joe believed that or he wouldn't be helping his wife out.

He and Edith had had thirty-six years together, and he hoped they had another thirty-six. They'd had hard times, of course, but everyone did. Edith had been his lover, his friend, his companion.

If Spence could find the same kind of life with Melanie, Joe would be satisfied.

"She seems the marrying kind," he said, an innocent look on his face.

"You'd think so," Spence returned.

"Problems in paradise?" Cal asked.

Joe watched his son struggle to come up with an answer.

Finally, Spence said, "Isn't there always a problem when a woman's involved?"

"I think that's a fair statement," Mac agreed.

"But you're a cynic," Cal pointed out.

"True." Mac did not argue.

"Well, I'm not," Spence said, sitting up straight, as if preparing for battle. "I'm going to marry and enjoy life, just like Cal."

"Whoa! I didn't say married life was easy." But Cal was grinning.

"But it's well worth it," Ed, his father, added.

"Yep," Joe agreed.

"Yeah," Spence said fervently.

Joe knew Edith was going to be thrilled.

THE FOUR WOMEN had carefully avoided the subject of their bet all evening. Finally, Ruth brought it up.

"Anyone have anything good to report?"

"About what?" Mabel asked, rearranging her cards.

"About the bet, of course. Tuck is out of town."

"Where?" Florence asked.

"Don't know. He said he'd be back Sunday or Monday."

Edith kept staring at her cards.

"What about you, Edith?" Ruth asked. "Is Spence showing any signs of—"

"No."

"I thought he liked that cute brunette working at

Jess's restaurant,'' Mabel said, frowning at her friend.

"He said she's in love with someone else. I don't want him to get married and be unhappy."

"No, that would be horrible," Florence agreed. "That's what happened to Mac."

"Does anyone know of any nice young ladies to introduce to him?" Edith asked hopefully.

They all solemnly shook their heads.

"Well," Edith said, "I've asked his father to talk to him. Maybe that will help."

"Those father-to-son talks never work," Mabel said. "Ed always beats around the bush so much that Cal can't figure out what he means."

"Do you remember when the boys asked Joe about sex after seeing the bull service a cow?" Ruth asked, a smile on her face. "They were only about four. It was before Mac came," she added for Florence's benefit.

They all laughed at that memory, but Edith's spirits weren't raised. She was worried about her son's future. Maybe Joe would have better luck.

JOE WAS WAITING for Edith when she got home that night. He couldn't wait to tell her her troubles were over.

"Guess what?"

"What, dear?" Edith asked as she removed her earrings.

"You don't have to worry about Spence anymore."

"I don't?" she asked in surprise, turning around to face him.

"Nope. That boy is as determined to marry as you are for him to do so."

"He is? You talked to him?"

"Didn't have to. He was with this pretty brunette. He couldn't keep his eyes off her. And at dinner, he told us he's going to get married. Her name's Melanie." He smiled triumphantly at his wife, sure he was about to receive a big hug.

"Oh, no!" Edith responded instead, suddenly sitting on the bed.

"Honey, what's wrong? I thought you'd be happy."

"I asked him about her the other day. But he said there was no chance because she was in love with someone else."

"Maybe she changed her mind."

"I don't think so. I could tell Spence was interested in her. I'm afraid she's taking him as second choice. Oh, Joe, I don't want that kind of marriage for Spence."

"Well, now, Edie, you don't know that."

"Oh, yes, I do. I can feel it here." She put her hand over her heart.

Feeling guilty, as if he'd caused this disaster, Joe tried to apologize.

"Oh, it's not your fault, dear." She got up and

began pacing the floor. "I have to do something. Only I don't know what."

Joe sighed. It was going to be a long night.

SPENCE WAITED for Melanie to get off work again.

"Spence, what are you doing?" she asked as she came from the back of the restaurant.

"I want to be sure you get home safely."

"It's just across the square, not a mile through the jungle," she said, smiling.

Ah, he loved her smile. "Indulge me, honey. I promise I won't ask to come in. But I want to be sure you're safe."

She didn't say anything else, which he took for acceptance and fell into step with her. After they came down the front steps, he took her hand in his.

"Done any more thinking about our earlier conversation?"

"No, I was too busy."

"So your answer is still no?"

"My answer to what?"

"To my marriage proposal."

"I don't remember a proposal. I remember you saying we'd be married, but no proposal."

"Is that why you said no?"

She smiled at him and he dropped her hand and put his arm around her shoulders.

"No. That would be a silly reason to turn you down."

"Another silly reason would be because you're pregnant."

She tried to pull away from his hold, but he didn't let her. "I've already told you, Spence. That's not a good reason to marry."

"I think the baby would think it's a good reason. If you'd had a choice, wouldn't you have wanted a daddy?"

She took in a deep breath, but she didn't answer him. "We're here. Thanks for walking me home."

"I'm seeing you upstairs."

Not arguing, she hurried up the stairs, as if anxious to get rid of him. And she probably was, because she didn't want to answer his question.

When she reached her door, she tried to dismiss him again. "Good night. Thank you—"

He wasn't interested in words anymore. He wanted to touch her, to feel her against him, to find the magic.

He slanted his mouth across hers and kissed her deeply, his hands stroking her, urging her ever closer, even though every inch of her was imprinted on his body now.

When his fingers slid beneath her sweater, coming in contact with soft, warm skin, he wanted to strip her naked there in the hall.

"Spence—" she began as his lips left hers to trace her jaw, but his mouth returned to hers. He didn't want to talk. She didn't fight him. In fact, her eagerness inspired him to greater heights. She opened up to him as she'd done at the wedding.

Suddenly she pushed against him. He relaxed his hold, not willing to force her. "Honey, let's go inside."

"No! You…you said you wouldn't ask to come in. We've made this mistake once, Spence. We can't do it again."

A mistake. She called their glorious lovemaking a mistake. "Why? We can't get you pregnant again."

She gave a brief chuckle, leaning her forehead against his shoulder. "No, we can't do that again. But we're not going to marry, we're not going to…to have sex again. You need to get on with your life. And the baby and I will be fine."

"Nope. You need to marry me, and the three of us will be fine."

"I can't do that, Spence."

"Why not?"

"Because a marriage without love won't work."

She was telling him again she loved Cal. Didn't she realize he'd never marry her? He and Jess were made for each other.

"Please, I need to go to bed. I'm exhausted."

He knew she was tired. He'd been raised to be a gentleman, so all he could do was leave. But he wasn't giving up.

"Okay, I'll leave. If you give me one more kiss."

She swallowed, looking a little panicked. "You promise?"

"I promise." His heart sang when her arms slid up his chest, her hands linking behind his neck, and she leaned into him. He took his kiss, one that would keep him up a long time that night, but it would be worth the lack of sleep.

As THEY CAME OUT of church the next morning, Edith turned to her husband. "I forgot to put something in the oven for dinner. Would you take me to The Last Roundup?"

"Now, Edie, I don't think—"

She glared at him. "As much as I've cooked for you all these years, I can't believe you're refusing to take me out to eat."

"Edie, you know that's not true. I'm worried about what you're going to do."

She stared at him, daring him to refuse her again— which, of course, he didn't.

When they reached the restaurant, Melanie Rule was working as hostess, as Edith had expected. Such a lovely girl. It was too bad.

"Melanie, hello," she said, smiling.

"Hello, Mrs. Hauk, Mr. Hauk. I should have a table for you in just a minute."

Melanie hoped she had a table for the Hauks. She certainly didn't want any more conversation with them. She checked with the waitresses and found a table available.

"This way, please."

After seating them, she handed them the menus and prepared to leave.

"Melanie, dear, could you get a short break?" Edith asked. "I'd like to talk with you for a minute."

"Possibly. I'll ask Jessica if she can cover for me."

"Thank you, dear."

Melanie went into the kitchen to find Jessica, wondering what Spence's mother wanted. Surely he hadn't told her about the baby. Or had Jerry told someone and word had gotten back to the Hauks?

"Jess, could you cover for me for about ten minutes? Mrs. Hauk needs to talk to me."

"Sure. Is everything okay?"

"I don't know. I'll hurry," she added with a smile before she went over to their table.

"Is now all right, Mrs. Hauk?"

"Yes, thank you. It's perfect." She looked across at her husband. "Excuse yourself, please, Joe."

"Edie, don't—"

His wife glared at him and he stopped midsentence and slid out of the booth.

Now Melanie was really worried if it was something Joe Hauk couldn't hear. She took his place in the booth and looked at Spence's mother.

"Dear, I want to ask you not to marry my son."

Chapter Seven

"Mom, what are you doing?" Spence's voice boomed as he came to a halt by the booth where Melanie and his mother were sitting. The instant he'd entered the restaurant and spotted the two women together, he'd known it could only mean trouble.

Edith seemed unable to speak, but Melanie slid out of the booth and faced Spence. "I don't think you should speak to your mother like that. We were having a little talk, not trying to overthrow the government."

"And what were you talking about?" Spence demanded, moving closer to Melanie.

She raised her chin and glared at him. "We were discussing how bright your future looks."

"Oh? Mom, what does she mean?" He knew he wasn't going to get anything out of Melanie, particularly here in public. His mother was another thing.

"Why…why, I was explaining to Melanie that I hope you marry some day to someone who truly loves you, and you have a lot of children." She gave him a wavery smile.

He looked at Melanie again and noted a sympathetic smile she sent his mother. "And what did you say, Melanie?"

"It's none of your business, but I wished your mother good luck. Now, if you'll excuse me, I need to get back to work."

She walked away without looking back, but Spence wanted more answers. He'd deal with Melanie when she got off work. He turned back to his mother. "Now let's hear what you really said."

Joe sat down across from his wife. "You'd better tell him, Edie."

"I told her I didn't want you to marry her. And she wasn't upset. She said she wasn't going to." Edith reached out for her son's hand. "I didn't want you to have a lopsided marriage."

Spence ruefully shook his head. If his mother had known about the baby, things would be different. And he couldn't tell her. "I hope you didn't offend her, Mom, because she's going to be your daughter-in-law." He smiled slightly. "As soon as I can convince her, that is. And I think you just made the convincing a little more difficult."

"Spence, dear, please don't—"

"Edie, you've interfered enough. Leave the boy alone," Joe advised.

"I just want you to be happy," she said to Spence.

"Me, too. So don't help me."

He walked back to the front of the restaurant, try-ing to figure out what to say to Melanie. But he didn't get a chance to speak to her. Cal had come in and was waiting for him.

"Jess says you're joining us."

"Yeah. I've decided I can't let the two of you eat a single meal alone. If I don't distract Jess, she might figure out you're not good enough for her." He grinned at his friend who took his teasing in stride.

The two of them walked to their special table and sat.

"Is something wrong?" Cal asked.

"Oh, yeah. Mom decided to talk to Melanie. She told her she didn't want us to get married." Spence buried his head in his hands.

"Hey, been there, done that."

"Don't tell me your mother didn't want you two married, Cal. I know better," Spence said, looking up at his friend.

"You're right. She wanted Jess pregnant, knowing I'd marry her at once. So she provided condoms that had been, uh, damaged." Cal stared into space, a smile on his lips. Then he shook his head. "So, you see, it could be worse. You could have gotten a lady pregnant before you knew what you were doing."

Spence figured he was about to spill the beans. He couldn't help himself. But the gods smiled on him when Tuck's arrival distracted him.

"Got room for me?"

"Sit down, tell us where you've been," Cal encouraged, pulling out a chair for him. "We missed you yesterday."

"Are you okay?" Spence asked. Somehow his own misery seemed to find a friend in Tuck's expression.

"Yeah, I'm fine," Tuck said, his voice almost defiant as he straddled the chair. He took off his cowboy hat and hung it on the back of his chair. "But I'm hungry enough to eat the biggest steak Jess has. Have you two ordered?"

"No, we're waiting on Jess," Cal assured him.

Tuck slumped down in his chair. "Anything happen here this weekend?"

Spence and Cal exchanged a look. Then Cal said, "Not really. Where did you go?"

"Dallas."

"That's quite a drive," Spence said.

"Yeah. And not worth it." He shrugged his shoulders. "I think I'm cured of my restlessness."

Spence and Cal exchanged another look.

"Did you see Alex while you were there?" Cal asked, naming the beautiful, blond attorney who represented Jessica in her restaurant sales.

Tuck shook his head and rearranged the silverware on the table.

Spence sighed. "Life is—"

"Spence? You're not mad at your mama, are you? She's real worried," Joe Hauk had suddenly appeared at their table.

Spence rubbed his forehead. "No, Dad, but tell her…tell her to not interfere again."

"I will, son. Goodbye," he ended, giving them all a little wave and rejoining Edith at the front of the restaurant.

"What was that all about?" Tuck asked.

Cal came to Spence's rescue. "It's about that stupid bet our mothers made. Spence's mom tried to—"

"Get him married off?"

Spence shook his head. "No, she told Melanie Rule *not* to marry me."

"What? That doesn't make sense. I thought they were all out to get us married."

"Get who married?" Mac asked, walking up.

Cal laughed. "Who else? The four of us. Join us, Mac."

"Are we having trouble with our mothers again?" Mac asked as he accepted Cal's invitation.

"Here and there," Cal answered.

Spence didn't say anything. Neither did Tuck.

Jessica arrived and glared at Spence. Cal pulled out the chair beside him for her, but she didn't even acknowledge her husband. "What did you say to Melanie?"

"Why?" Spence asked, leaning forward even as his gaze darted to the front of the restaurant.

"She's upset."

"She's crying?" Spence asked, rising to his feet.

"No, she's not crying. But she's not happy."

Lunch held no interest for Spence now. He walked

to the front of the restaurant, leaving his friends behind, just barely hearing Tuck's question.

"What the hell is going on here?"

When he got to the front of the restaurant, that same question occurred to Spence. Melanie wasn't there. One of the waitresses was filling in as hostess and said Melanie had gone home.

He hurried to her apartment, but she wouldn't answer the door, if she was there. He finally went home and called several times, but she never answered the phone. In spite of his frustration, he decided he should avoid Melanie until he had a plan of action.

One that would guarantee his winning.

AFTER WORKING ALL DAY Monday, on horseback, thankfully, instead of walking, Spence was ready with a plan. He conferred with Maria, cleaned up, and headed for town.

He would've liked to sit in on Melanie's meeting with the Poindexters and Mac, but he knew better than to ask. But he was going to be at Cal's office at five.

When he got there, he found his friend finishing up some paperwork. "Howdy, Cal. Has Melanie shown up yet?"

"Well, good to see you, too," Cal teased. "Can't you think about anything but Melanie?"

"Guess not," Spence said with a shrug. He was through hiding his intent as far as Melanie was concerned. It was time for an all-out assault.

Cal's eyebrows soared. "New approach?"

"Damn right."

"Well, she should be—"

As if his words had conjured her up, Melanie tapped on Cal's door and he greeted her. "Melanie! I'll be ready in just a minute."

"No, Cal, I'm going to have to beg off."

She hadn't seen Spence until he moved to her side. "You mean, you're not going to Jess's party?"

Melanie stepped back. "I didn't see you, Spence. Um, yes, that's right. I'm not going."

"Are you feeling all right?"

"Of course," she assured him, squaring her shoulders. "But...but I'm not in a party mood. Will you give my apologies to Jess?" she asked Cal.

Spence studied her. Her gaze wouldn't connect with his, and her lips drooped at the corners. Something had gone wrong. And he wasn't about to let her get away without telling him.

He took hold of Melanie's arm and spoke to Cal. "Tell Jess we'll be a little late, but we'll show."

"No, I—"

Remembering his new approach, Spence bent and stopped her protest with his lips. When he straightened, both he and Melanie were breathing rapidly and her cheeks were bright red. Over his shoulder, he said, "Later," and pulled Melanie from Cal's office.

"Spence, what's gotten into you? You can't—"

"Yes, I can. I want to help you. Are you changing before we go?"

"Go where?"

"To my place. I suddenly remembered you hadn't seen my home, so I asked my housekeeper to fix dinner for us. Maria is so excited, she's been cooking since noon."

"Spence, I can't go to your house for dinner."

"You know, I love Jess's restaurant, but I've eaten there so many times the past few days that Maria was refusing to speak to me. The only way to redeem myself was to bring a guest so she could cook for someone besides me. Please?"

All the while, he was moving them in the direction of her apartment. When they reached the downstairs door, she looked at him. "Why are we here?"

"I didn't know if you'd need to change before we go. If not, my truck is right here."

"I can't— I'm not in a party mood."

"I know. And I'm trying to be patient. When we get to the ranch, you'll have some quiet time, and we can talk about what went wrong."

She turned big eyes on him. "You don't have to do this."

"I know, but I want to. Go get ready. I'll wait down here for fifteen minutes. If you're not down by then, I'll come get you." He watched her as she climbed the stairs, finding the view most appealing. She was dressed in a business suit, the most formal clothing he'd seen her wear.

And she still looked good.

Fourteen minutes later, she came down in a short black skirt, black hose that made her legs look a mile long, and a silk, long-sleeved blouse. He surprised her by greeting her with a kiss.

"You...you really should stop doing that. People are going to talk," she protested.

"I hope so. Come on." Taking her hand, he led her to his pickup and helped her in. When he sat behind the wheel, he immediately initiated a simple conversation, to take her mind from her troubles.

"Do you like the country? I never asked, but you were raised somewhere else, weren't you?"

"I was raised in Lubbock, but I prefer life in Cactus. It's nicer, more personal."

"I like it, too. Do you ride?"

"Uh, no, I never have."

He couldn't imagine life without horses. "Not now, but after the baby's born, I'll teach you. I've got a gentle mare named Cupcake that will be perfect for you."

"Cupcake?" Melanie asked, a smile on her face for the first time. "I thought cowboys named their horses things like Thunder or Devil. Something fierce."

"I guess I'm not the fierce type."

She slanted him a look out of the corner of her eye. "Oh, you've appeared rather fierce to me on occasion."

He shrugged, grinning. "You bring out the best in me."

They drove along in silence until she asked, "Do you have cows on your place?"

He chuckled, "Honey, it wouldn't be much of a ranch without those ornery critters. We run a couple of thousand head."

"Two thousand cows?" she asked, startled. "How do you keep track of all of them?"

"I don't do it by myself. We've got ten thousand acres, so I have four men who work for me. And we use four-wheel-drive vehicles and a small plane, as well as horses."

"But I thought—I mean, I heard you were wealthy, and I thought you just played at ranching."

He pulled into the long drive that led to the ranch house. "If this is playing, I sure don't want to face hard work."

By the time he got around the truck, after parking, to help her, she was already out of it. "By the way," he said, lowering his voice, "I hope you like tamales, because Maria makes the best there is, and she'll be disappointed if you don't."

"Why, yes, I love them, but I feel bad that she went to all this trouble."

Spence grinned, remembering Maria's excitement when he told her he was bringing his future wife for dinner. "She's not complaining."

He could hardly wait to get through the introductions and sit to eat with Melanie. He was anxious to know what had caused her to withdraw. When Maria finally left them alone, he didn't hesitate to go straight to his questioning. "Okay, what went wrong today? Was Jerry difficult?"

"No. Since you threatened him—" she paused to grin at him "—he's been most cooperative."

"Then it must've been your meeting with the Poindexters. Didn't Mac do a good job?"

"Mac was wonderful. We'd worked out an offer that was fair to all of us, and the Poindexters agreed that it was a good offer." She kept her head down, pretending to focus on the plate of food before her. But he noticed she wasn't eating much.

"Then what went wrong?"

She squared her shoulders and looked at him, a calm smile on her face. He wondered if she ever let down her guard. "I seem to have one flaw that the Poindexters couldn't accept."

He knew he was prejudiced. He'd been thinking of Melanie as perfect for a number of months now. But he couldn't imagine anything that would preclude doing business with her.

"They had a problem with you?" he asked incredulously.

Her smile widened. "Thanks, Spence. You've made me feel better."

"Hell, that shop of theirs is a disaster. They should get down on their knees and give thanks that they got any kind of offer."

"Well, I *was* feeling better," she said with an impish grin.

He thought about how his words could've been taken, and he grinned back. "I'm not the soul of tact, by the way. You'd better know that up front."

She looked down at her food, then back at Spence. "I know you're a good friend. That counts more than anything."

"So tell me what the problem is," he insisted, but her words sang in his heart.

"I'm single."

He waited, but she said nothing else, taking a bite of her tamales.

"That's it? You're not married?"

"That's it." She batted her eyelashes like an old-time Southern belle. "You know us weak little women need a strong man to guide us."

Spence threw his head back and roared with laughter. "Oh, my, they're not good judges of character, are they?"

"Nor do they live in the twentieth century," Melanie concluded with a sigh.

"Are you going to give up?" Somehow he couldn't see that happening. Not strong, determined Melanie.

She didn't answer at once. Finally she raised her gaze from the plate of food and said, "No. I'm not giving up on my idea. But I have to give up on that spot."

"Tell me about your idea."

She hesitated. "Do you really want to know, because sometimes I get carried away when I talk about it."

He could listen to her talk all night, about anything, but he needed to know about her dreams.

"Yeah, I really want to know."

She talked for almost half an hour about converting the sad Resale Shop into a modern consignment store that honored the past with its inventory but presented it in bright, pleasant surroundings.

When she finally ran out of things to tell him, she'd completely cleaned her plate and laughter was in her eyes again. Spence was pleased.

"Well, I'm impressed, Mel. I think you can make a go of your shop."

She sent him a grateful smile. "Thanks, but I guess my timing's wrong."

"Your timing is perfect. And I have a solution for your problem." And his. He couldn't wait to tell her.

Chapter Eight

"A solution?" A hopeful light sparked her eyes, then faded. "Thanks, but Mac told me there's not anything to do. Legally, they can lease to whomever they choose."

"Mac doesn't have my resources," Spence teased with a smile.

She stiffened. "If you're going to offer me money, please don't. I can't take it."

"Of course not. Money wouldn't fix your problem. But marriage will."

She stared at him. "Don't be silly."

"I'm not. Want to walk out to the barn and meet Cupcake?" He smiled when she seemed taken aback by his change of subject.

"Okay."

As they passed through the kitchen, she offered Maria several compliments about the meal and even offered to help with the dishes, which, of course, Maria declined. As they continued out the back door,

Spence looked back at his housekeeper to receive her nod of approval.

"Maria likes you," he announced as they headed to the barn.

"How do you know?"

"She just told me. And think how much time she's going to save you."

"How will Maria save me time?"

"She'll do all the cooking and cleaning. Between the store and being pregnant, you'll need all your energy." Everything was working out fine.

"What are you talking about?" Melanie demanded, coming to an abrupt halt and glaring at him.

He took her arm and urged her forward, but she didn't budge. Stubborn...and beautiful...woman. "See, when we marry and you move into the house, you won't have to worry about—"

"Wait just a minute. We're not getting married. I told you that, and your mother—"

"Has nothing to do with it. Look, here's the deal. I want to marry you so I can be a father to my child, so my child won't be a bastard. You want to marry so you can have your shop."

"You think I would marry for financial advantage?" she asked, her voice rising.

"A lot of people do, honey, probably more than we realize, but no, I don't think you would. Not for that reason alone. But it would be best for both of us, and most especially, it would be best for our child."

She turned away, crossing her arms around her middle. "Spence, I don't want my child to be illegitimate, but I also don't want her to have to deal with a divorce. Or a daddy who doesn't want to be there."

He put his arm around her shoulders and urged her toward the barn. Holding her close to him, he whispered, "I want to be there, Mel. I really want to."

"You'd feel trapped."

They entered into the shadowy barn and he led her to the stall where he'd had Maria's husband put Cupcake just after they arrived. The horse immediately came over to be petted as soon as she saw Spence.

"Rub her nose. She won't bite."

After a doubtful glance at him, Melanie reached out and rubbed her fingers across Cupcake's nose. "It's like velvet!" she exclaimed.

"Yeah. We can make a special agreement that if either one of us wants to leave before the baby's born, we can." He turned her to look at him. "That way no one will feel trapped."

"The trapped part comes after the baby arrives," she assured him with dryness.

"Why are you so sure about this?"

She looked away from him. Finally she said, "My daddy taught me that lesson well. And my mother explained it to me over and over again."

"What did she explain?"

"That men resent being trapped by crying babies. They leave and don't come back."

"Because your mom said it doesn't make it so. Not everyone is like your dad."

She looked away, and he tenderly tucked a strand of brown hair behind her ear. "That must've been hard, honey, but you can't let it ruin your life."

Her chin came up. "I'm not. I told you the baby and I will be fine."

"But you'd be better with a husband, a daddy. We'd be a family."

"I don't have any experience with family," she said with a bitter laugh. "I just had my mom…and the guilt she heaped on me."

"Seems like a big burden for a little girl to bear," he whispered.

When she turned to him, there was a question in her gaze, and he couldn't hold back the urge to kiss her. Pulling her against him, his lips covered hers with a gentle touch, as if stroking them to life. Her breath caught before she relaxed against him, and the kiss grew more urgent.

He wrapped his arms tightly around her, his hands tracing her body, stroking and defining every part of her. When he detected the smallest bulge at her waist, he released her and pulled back in wonder. "Is that the baby?"

Her gaze was almost shy as she glanced up at him before nodding. He pulled her against him, burying her face against his neck. "I want to strip you naked and love every inch of you. I want—"

She pushed out of his hold. "I think you'd better slow down, cowboy. We're not— I haven't—"

He grinned, refusing to be discouraged. "Nope, you haven't. But we're making progress. And we can go at whatever speed you want, Mel, as long as we get married at once."

"What?" she asked, stepping back and bumping into the stable door. Cupcake nosed her arm, startling her. "Oh! Oh, Cupcake, I'm sorry, I—"

"She just wants some attention," he assured her. Taking a step closer to her, he added, "So do I."

Melanie held up a hand to keep him at arm's length. "Spence, you're moving too fast."

"Time and babies wait for no man, honey. I want us married before everyone realizes you're pregnant. And the Poindexters might find someone else to lease their store to. You wouldn't want that to happen."

"You wouldn't have a problem with me opening my store?" she asked, a hint of surprise in her voice.

If she'd asked that question a week ago, Spence would have insisted *his* wife wouldn't work. But he'd learned Melanie was an independent lady. He was willing to make some changes if it would convince her to marry him.

"You'll have to have something to do. Of course, you'll need to quit your jobs, and be sure you get enough rest, but I know you have to make your own decisions."

"Then why did *you* decide I'd quit my jobs?"

He rolled his eyes. "Okay, I'd *suggest* you quit

your jobs. After all, I'd pay our living expenses. I'd be the husband.''

"So women don't contribute to the finances?''

"Well, I guess some of them do.''

"Like Jessica?''

"Yeah, but—wait a minute! Why are we fighting about this?''

She shrugged her shoulders and turned to pet Cupcake again. "She's very sweet.''

"Yeah. So, do we tell everyone tonight we're getting married?''

With an exasperated look, she said, "No, we don't. Nothing's been decided.''

"But, honey, I promised we'd take things slow. I mean, I'd understand if you didn't want to, you know, share a bed right away, but—''

"Share a bed? You mean—'' She turned a bright red. "I'm going to get fat. You don't want to have sex with me.''

He smiled at her, his hands reaching out to pull her against him again. "I can't imagine wanting anyone more than I want you. Don't you remember how it was for us at Cal's wedding?''

"That was an accident,'' she whispered, leaning her forehead against his shoulder.

"I've got a bed upstairs if you want to lay money on that theory. I wouldn't mind showing you something special happened last time and will happen again. Can't you tell that when we kiss?''

"It's just a…a chemical reaction or something.''

His embrace tightened and a grin settled on his face. "Man, if we bottle and sell it, we'll be rich."

She pushed away from him. "You already are. Are we going to the party?"

"I'd rather try out the bed."

"I need to powder my nose before we go," she said stubbornly, her gaze meeting his.

With a sigh, he swept his arm toward the barn door. "After you, honey. You can have some time to think. I'll let you stew until Friday, but earlier would be better."

"Spence, I haven't promised anything."

"I know, but Junior and I only have so much patience. And to be democratic, two out of three is a majority." He shot her a hopeful grin as they walked out into the evening light.

With an exasperated look, she said, "Number One, you don't know that this baby is a boy. And Number Two, you don't know that the baby would vote your way."

His gaze turned serious. "Oh, yes, I do. No baby would want to be without both his parents. The angels wouldn't let him vote any other way."

She looked down and said nothing until they'd reached the back porch. Then she tugged her hand from his and said, "I'll be ready in a minute."

MELANIE WAS RELIEVED to join other people. Spence on his own was too persuasive, whether he was using words or those incredible lips of his. She'd never responded to another man as she did to him.

"I'm glad you came," Jessica said as Melanie walked into the Baxter house.

"I'm sorry I wasn't here earlier to help you."

"Mac said you got some bad news."

Melanie grimaced. "I guess you could say that. Or at least, a postponement." She told her about the consignment store and the Poindexters' objections.

Jessica's indignation was soothing. "I can't believe anyone could be so out-of-date. Can't you sue them?"

"Mac said no."

"Well, then, you'll just have to get married." Jessica said it as if she were suggesting Melanie change her blouse.

Laughter bubbled up in Melanie. Without thinking, she said, "You and Spence. I didn't realize you thought alike."

"Aha! I knew there was something going on between the two of you," Jess exclaimed.

"Oh, no! I didn't mean— That is—"

Spence stepped to her side, sliding his arm around her. "What's up, honey? Is Jess harassing you?"

By now, Melanie was so embarrassed she didn't think she could face anyone. "Tell Jess we're not— there's nothing going on," she whispered, leaning toward Spence.

As Cal joined them, Spence pulled her completely

against him and grinned as he said, "Well, now, honey, I can't tell a lie."

"Spence!" Melanie said with a gasp.

Cal attempted to lessen her embarrassment. "It's okay, Melanie. We all know Spence is crazy about you."

All those standing around laughed, but Melanie lifted her gaze and encountered a sad look on Edith Hauk's face as she watched them from across the room. Suddenly she was reminded that she wasn't the only one who didn't want this marriage. Or shouldn't want it.

"Um, could I have some more peach tea, Jess? It's really good." Anything to escape being the center of attention.

As if she understood, Jessica took her arm. "Of course, come with me." She led the way into the kitchen.

"Thank you," Melanie muttered as the door closed behind them. "It was a little crowded in there."

"Don't mind the teasing. It's just that everyone loves Spence and we all would like to see him happy." She took a pitcher from the refrigerator. "Did you really want tea, Melanie, or did you want to escape those guys?"

"Both. The tea really is good." Of course, she suffered from a pregnant woman's need to frequently excuse herself and the tea didn't help.

Jessica sighed. "I love it, too, but I can't drink too

much right now or I'd spend all evening in the—''
She suddenly broke off and busied herself pouring
Melanie's tea.

If she weren't pregnant herself, Melanie would
never have realized what Jessica meant. But she did.
''You're pregnant?'' she whispered.

Jessica immediately shushed her. ''No one knows.
Cal and I decided not to tell anyone because of the
stupid bet the ladies made.''

''Why? You've won.'' Melanie stared at her
blankly.

''I know, but— Wait a minute. How did you know
I was pregnant?''

Melanie turned a bright red and looked away.

''*You* can't be—are you? Who's the— Spence?
You're pregnant and Spence is the daddy?''

Melanie didn't know where to look. Finally she
nodded, but she hurriedly said, ''Don't tell anyone.''

''No, of course not. But when…how— We didn't
even realize you were dating.''

Melanie couldn't clam up now, but she didn't want
to go into the whole story of her and Spence at the
wedding. Especially not when it started with her having a crush on Jessica's husband. Instead she just
said, ''I-it happened…one night a few months ago.''

''Oh, Melanie, you poor dear. And Spence didn't
find out until last week? Friday? I guess he's demanding that you marry him.''

Melanie nodded.

"Why won't you?" Jessica asked, a worried frown on her face.

Melanie explained about her childhood and her mother's warnings, and her determination not to follow in her mother's footsteps. "We'll be fine, the baby and me."

Then Jessica asked a difficult question. "But how will Spence be?"

"Spence will have his freedom. He can fall in love with some lady and have the future he wants," Melanie assured Jessica, her chin up.

"It sure won't do his reputation much good, to know he fathered a child and didn't marry the mother."

Melanie hadn't thought about that aspect of their situation. Suddenly sad, she asked, "So you think I should leave?"

"No! But couldn't you consider marrying Spence? He's a good guy. And there must've been something between you for you to get pregnant in the first place."

Melanie's cheeks burned again. "He was comforting me."

"About what?"

"Oh! This is embarrassing," Melanie whispered. She took a sip of tea to cool herself off. Then, resolutely, she looked at Jessica. "I had a crush on Cal because—oh, I don't mean he isn't attractive—but he was safe. He couldn't be all those things my mother warned me about because he was a lawman, a good man. So I thought I could have my dreams if I chose someone like that."

Jessica seemed taken aback for a moment. Then she nodded. "That makes sense. But you're not still—"

"No, I'm no martyr. Once I saw how he looked at you last October, I knew there was no hope. But Spence had figured out—at least, he realized I was attracted to Cal. At the wedding, I went and hid because...because I was losing my composure. That's when he found me."

"Does he think you still want Cal?"

"I don't know. We haven't talked about it."

The two ladies sat staring at each other. Then Jessica reached across the kitchen table to take Melanie's hands in hers and squeeze them. "Wow. This changes everything."

"It does?"

"Yes. You got pregnant on my wedding day. We used protection until that night, so we probably got pregnant on the same day."

Melanie didn't see the significance of Jessica's words. "What difference does that make?"

Jessica chuckled. "Ah. Of course, you haven't been exposed to the four ladies who plotted their sons' downfall."

"You mean, the bet about who would get a grandchild first?" Then, of course, Melanie realized what Jessica meant. "Oh! But no one will know—I mean, if I don't marry Spence—"

"If you don't marry Spence, Edith Hauk will never forgive you," Jessica assured her with a laugh.

"I think you're wrong. She told me she didn't want me marrying Spence."

That shocked Jessica. "Why—"

The swinging door came partway open and two men peeked through. Cal asked, "What's going on in here?"

Jessica smiled at her husband. "We're telling secrets."

"What kind of secrets?" Spence demanded, alarm on his face.

"Later," Jess assured him with a smile as she strolled past him back to the living room.

Cal, with a raised eyebrow, stared at the other two, then followed Jessica.

"What's going on, Melanie?" Spence asked, moving closer to her.

"N-nothing," she assured him even as she sped past him before he could stop her. In thirty seconds, he stood alone in the kitchen, no more knowing of what had just happened than he'd been before he came in.

Chapter Nine

"Good night, and thank you for coming," Jessica called to the last of her departing guests. Except for Spence and Melanie. They'd actually tried to excuse themselves once, but Jess had stopped them with a look.

She shut the door and turned to face her captive audience. "Okay, get comfortable and let's talk."

Spence tried, again. "Look, Jess, it's late and I know you're tired. Why don't we—"

"Nope. You know what Melanie told me, don't you?"

Cal looked at him in surprise. "You mean you know—"

"Hell, yes, I know!" Spence roared. "Don't you think I should?"

"Well, of course, but I haven't told Tuck and Mac, so—"

"I would hope you haven't!" Spence returned.

"Well, I would!" Cal raised his voice. "I don't want anyone to think I'm not happy about the baby."

"Thanks, but I don't think—"

"Thanks? Why would you thank me? It's my baby!"

"It is not! She may have— I mean, it's my baby! I can't believe you'd say that in front of Jessica!"

The two men were standing nose to nose, their hands on their hips, until they noticed Jessica rolling on the couch with hysterical laughter.

"Wait a minute," Cal said, frowning. "What's so funny, baby?"

Melanie sat by herself on the other sofa, staring at her hands clasped tightly in her lap. Spence couldn't read anything from her expression.

Jessica sat up, wiping her eyes. "Guys, you are so funny. But I think I can ease everything if I tell you there are two babies."

Cal turned to stare at Melanie while Spence did the same to Jessica. "You're pregnant?" they both asked simultaneously.

Both ladies nodded, Jessica proudly and Melanie with determination.

Then the men looked at each other before they wrapped each other in a congratulatory bear hug.

"Now do you see why we need to talk?" Jessica asked, patting the sofa beside her. "Come on, Cal, sit down. You, too, Spence."

Spence didn't need any urging to take his place beside Melanie. He'd scarcely gotten close to her all evening.

The logistics were the first things on Cal's mind.

"But you two haven't shown any interest in each other until the last few days. How could you already be pregnant?"

"Gee, Cal," Jessica drawled. "That was so tactfully put. If we made you ambassador, we could have another war on our hands."

"Well, baby, you'll have to admit—"

"It was at your wedding," Spence said abruptly.

"What was?" Cal asked, losing track of his original question.

"When Melanie got pregnant."

Cal blinked several times, then grinned at Spence. "Well, I'll be damned. The baby race is on."

"What do you mean?" Spence asked.

"We figure that's when Jessica got pregnant, too."

Spence shook his head. "Lordy, lordy, we're in for it now."

"How long can we keep it a secret?" Cal asked his wife.

"At least another couple of months, I hope," Jessica said, her hands coming to rest on her still flat stomach. "With the first one, I've read, the lady doesn't show as quickly."

Spence sent a furtive glance to Melanie's trim figure. Only by touching her had he felt a difference in her figure. "Uh-oh," he said, suddenly remembering, "Jerry knows."

Jessica stared at Melanie. "You told Jerry?"

Melanie continued to remain silent.

"It's my fault. She asked to go to another town to

get her prescription filled, but I insisted—I thought she was trying to hide, I mean, I thought—''

Melanie reached out and touched his arm and Spence subsided. But he also took her hand in his and wouldn't let go.

Cal smugly looked at his friend. "We took our prescription to Muleshoe," he said, naming a nearby town.

"Quit bragging. That was my idea," Jessica reminded him with a laugh.

"Do you think Jerry will keep it quiet?" Cal asked, returning to the problem at hand.

Spence squared his jaw. "He'd better. I'll have a talk with him tomorrow."

"Did anyone see you in Doc's office?" Jessica asked. "We went afterhours."

Melanie chewed on her bottom lip.

Spence was beginning to feel like the most hamfisted, bungling oaf in history. He'd forced Melanie into visiting Doc in the middle of the day, when his office was full. "I didn't think."

Melanie spoke for the first time. "If anyone asks, I can say I had the flu."

"Or that you were getting a prescription for birth control pills," Jessica added. "Of course, that would crush your mother," she said, looking at Spence. "And she doesn't seem happy as it is. What does she have against Melanie?"

Melanie stiffened and tried harder to free her hand.

"Honey, it's not you," Spence hurriedly said.

"It's me, again. I don't seem to have done anything right lately."

"What do you mean?" Melanie asked, leaning toward him.

He liked the sweet concern he saw in her gaze. As a reward, he snatched a quick kiss, which had her pulling at her hand again. "I told her you were in love with someone else. She was afraid I'd be unhappy if we got married."

"You will be," she whispered. "A marriage based only on a baby is a disaster."

Cal leaned forward. "Are you in love with someone else?"

Spence felt Melanie's agony as her cheeks flamed. But he stared as much as the other two when Melanie shook her head no.

Wait a minute. Was she lying to protect herself from further embarrassment? Of course she was. And he didn't blame her. It was an embarrassing situation.

Jessica answered Cal's question. "She had a crush on someone, but she doesn't any longer."

Spence stared at Jessica. "She told you?" He turned back to stare at Melanie, who continued to keep her gaze fixed on her feet.

"That's not the point," Jessica said calmly. "We need to decide if we're going to announce our pregnancies now, or wait a while. I vote for waiting until we have to. I think it might be fun to see if Mac and Tuck's parents can pull off a—what do you call when there are four? A trifecta is three. Would it be a quatrifecta? Is there such a thing?''

"Baby, it doesn't much matter what you call it. It isn't going to happen,'' Cal assured her.

"I don't know,'' Jessica said, grinning at her husband. "When I first heard of the bet, I didn't give it a chance to work on even one of you staunch bachelors. Now there's a fifty percent success rate. Pretty impressive.''

"Yeah, but Mac isn't going to marry—or get anyone pregnant,'' Cal added, slanting a grin at Spence. "He's very careful. And I don't know what's going on with Tuck, but the way he acted tonight, he's looking for quantity, not quality.''

Silence fell as they contemplated their friends. Then Jessica spoke. "Oh, well, what's it to be? What do you want to do, guys?'' she asked, looking at Spence and Melanie.

Spence turned to Melanie, but she didn't look up. And she didn't look comfortable. He turned to his friends. "Well, the biggest decision I see isn't when to tell, but what to tell. Until Melanie agrees to marry me, I don't have any announcements I want to make.''

"You haven't convinced her yet?'' Cal asked incredulously.

"She thinks I'll be unhappy,'' Spence muttered, his gaze returning to Melanie.

Jessica left Cal's side to take Melanie's other hand. "Melanie, for the sake of the baby, I think you should marry Spence at least until it's born. I was an illegitimate baby. I wouldn't want my child to have to carry that label, even today."

Melanie looked at Jessica in surprise. "I didn't know."

"I was very lucky. Not only was my mother strong, like you are, but I also had Cal's friendship. He became my protector. People didn't dare insult me because they knew Cal would beat them up. But I knew. Inside, I knew I was different from everyone else."

Melanie took a deep breath that was more like a sob to Spence's ears. He dropped her hand and wrapped his arm around her shoulders. "It's okay, Mel, don't cry."

"No, I won't cry. But…but I don't know what to do. I want my baby to be happy."

"Our baby is going to be happy because we're both going to be there for him, married or not. But I think he'd be happier if we're married."

"She, not he," she said, but Spence thought her reminder was automatic.

"Whichever," he told her with a grin.

Cal put in his two cents' worth. "I agree with Spence. And, Melanie, he's a man of his word."

Spence didn't know which words were the most persuasive, but he didn't care. Melanie raised her gaze to his and murmured the most precious word he'd ever heard. "Okay."

MELANIE LAY IN BED the next morning, wondering what she'd agreed to. She should've waited until today to make her decision. She'd been swayed by the emotions of the moment. Swayed by Jessica's words, Cal's reassurance, and most of all, by Spence.

Damn! She was going to commit a double mistake, according to her mother. She'd gotten pregnant by the man…and she had lost her heart to him.

He was so sweet, so supportive. Not always making the right decision, but never backing down. Never going away. Of course, they'd only been talking again since Friday. But he'd tried to establish a relationship with her after the wedding.

She'd been too scared. Scared of her response to him. Embarrassed that she'd abandoned her principles in a split second. Afraid he considered her easy game.

She dismissed that thought, since it was too late now, and returned to the more urgent one. Last night, on the way home, Spence had wanted to discuss details. But she'd pleaded exhaustion.

Immediately, he'd pulled her to his side, wrapped his arm around her and told her to rest.

How could she resist such sweetness? She'd laid her head on his shoulder, planning on pretending to sleep so she wouldn't have to make any more decisions. Instead, he'd had to awaken her when they reached the apartment.

But now she had to face her decision. And she was scared.

Even as she realized that thought, her stomach told her it wasn't a happy one, and she raced to the bathroom.

An hour later she ran into the drugstore, almost late, knowing she didn't look her best. Jerry's eagle eye was on her as she sped down the aisle, but she reached the time clock just as the minute hand struck eight. She threw her belongings in the small room they ludicrously called the employee lounge and rushed back into the store to begin work.

"Good morning, Melanie," Jerry said formally. He'd been scrupulously polite since his encounter with Spence.

"Good morning, Jerry," she returned and began stocking the shelves with the delivery that had come in last night.

The manual work, needing little thought, was soothing, and after half an hour, Melanie's stomach began to settle and she thought she'd be able to make it through the day.

The bell jingled over the door. She looked up, a smile on her face, ready to greet a customer. Instead, all she could see was a huge arrangement of long-stemmed red roses. The man holding the flowers walked forward and she realized it was Mickey Blankenship, the owner of the one florist shop in town.

"Melanie Rule?" he asked, stopping in front of her.

She nodded.

"I thought that was you. Look what I have for

you. These were just shipped in this morning in preparation for Valentine's Day. I sure didn't think I'd be delivering them today, but then, you never know. Aren't you a lucky lady?''

The lady who worked behind the soda fountain, Lucy, came rushing over. "Oh, Melanie! Who are they from? Aren't they beautiful? I've never seen such pretty roses.''

Jerry also came forward. "You're supposed to be working, Melanie, not taking personal time.''

Mickey frowned at the owner. "Come on, Jerry, give the lady a break. It's not every day anyone gets a gift like these. Cost a pretty penny, too, let me tell you,'' he ended, laughing with excitement.

"Hon, would you like to put them on the end of the lunch counter? That way, everyone can see them,'' Lucy suggested.

Oh, good. Just what she wanted. "Uh, I—"

"That's a great idea,'' Mickey agreed. "And everyone will see my tag on the flowers and know where to come if they want the same thing.''

Melanie could practically see dollar signs ringing in his eyes as he beamed at her.

Still, she wasn't prepared to advertise anything because she knew it would draw a lot of questions, questions she didn't want to answer. She opened her mouth to refuse Lucy's offer when the bell over the door jingled again.

The sudden fear that Spence might have followed his roses froze her.

"Hi, Mac," Jerry said, his voice suddenly showing a nervousness that in other circumstances might have amused Melanie.

All she felt now was relief. It wasn't Spence.

"Hey, you never did say who sent these," Lucy pointed out as Mac came to stand beside Melanie. "Was it you, Mac Gibbons? Are you courting our Melanie? Flo will be so happy."

"No, it's not me," Mac said with a smile. "But I did come to talk to Melanie. Jerry, mind if we have a couple of minutes to chat?"

Jerry suddenly became the magnanimous employer. "No, of course not. Take all the time you need."

Mac took Melanie's arm and led her to the back of the store where Jerry had a couple of chairs for those who had to wait for prescriptions.

"Wait!" Melanie called, and hurried back to Mickey and the bouquet of flowers. She carefully unpinned the card, then opened it. Spence had signed his name but that was all. What had she hoped for? A declaration of love? She put the card in her pocket and hurried back to Mac.

Lucy took the flowers from Mickey and carried them to the soda counter, displaying them prominently. Melanie watched her with a sigh.

"Melanie?" Mac said, drawing her attention. "I have good news. Spence called me this morning and told me I could tell the Poindexters about your marriage. They were pleased and agreed to sign your offer at once.''

She stared at him, excitement, panic, anger, joy, all running around in her stomach. Then she leaped to her feet and rushed to the back of the store, hoping she made the ladies' room in time to avoid embarrassing herself in public.

SPENCE FROWNED as he came into the drugstore. Usually this early in the morning, there wasn't a lot of traffic.

When he identified Mickey Blankenship, he realized his gift to Melanie had been delivered. He hoped she was pleased.

Then Mac came from the back of the store. Had he already talked to Melanie? Spence had only talked to him half an hour ago, but he thought they should get the ball rolling.

Where was Melanie?

He started toward Mac but was interrupted by Jerry. "If you're here to see Melanie, she's in the back with Mac. I let her have time for a personal conference.''

The man acted as if he should be rewarded, Spence thought in disgust. But something more important was on his mind. "She's not with Mac. He's here. Mac, where's Melanie?''

"She got up and ran to the back of the store. I'm afraid she may be sick.''

Spence immediately started to go after her, but she

appeared suddenly, pale-faced, and walked toward them. She barely acknowledged his presence, a sure sign that she was upset. Instead, she turned her attention to Mac. "I apologize. I think I have a touch of the flu."

"Maybe you'd better sit down," Mac suggested.

Spence put his arm around her for support and felt her stiffen. Not a good sign.

"If Jerry doesn't mind, maybe you could take a break. We'll go sit down in a booth and get you a little soda to drink," he suggested, looking at Jerry.

"Mac, too?" Jerry blurted. His cheeks red, he added, "Of course. Take a break. I always take good care of my employees. Wouldn't want them working if they didn't feel well. You go ahead, Melanie. Feel free." He turned and almost ran back to the pharmacy counter.

"What's gotten into him?" Mac asked as he moved with Spence and Melanie to the side of the store.

Spence said nothing.

Melanie muttered, "Ask Spence."

Mac accepted Spence's quick shake of his head. They reached the booth and Melanie slid in with a thankful sigh. Mac sat opposite her.

"I'll get Melanie a soda," Spence said, and turned away.

"Hey, get me a cup of coffee, while you're at it."

"No!" Melanie protested at once.

Mac was startled. He stared at her, waiting.

Spence frantically tried to think of something to say, realizing Melanie's dilemma.

Melanie was quicker. "I'm sorry, Mac, it's just that the smell of coffee…it's so pungent…makes me more nauseated. If you—"

"No problem. I didn't think of that. I'll take a soda, too, Spence."

With a relieved sigh, he smiled at his friend. "Three sodas, coming right up."

He gave their order to Lucy and she insisted he go visit with his friends and she would bring their drinks. He decided that might be a good idea. Melanie seemed fragile this morning and Mac might ask the wrong question.

He slid in beside her, putting his right arm behind her on the back of the booth. "Lucy's bringing them. Why are you here, Mac?"

"Well, after you called me, I talked to the Poindexters and they were ready to sign on the dotted line. I wanted to tell Melanie."

"Oh, good. I'd hoped to talk to her before—I mean, I hadn't told her I was going to tell you," Spence explained. He was watching Melanie out of the corner of his eye. "It occurred to me this morning."

She still said nothing, remaining rigid in her corner.

"You are pleased, aren't you, Melanie?" Mac asked. "You still want the store, don't you? Oh, and by the way," he added with a grin, "congratulations, you two."

"Thank you," Melanie replied, sounding a little more composed. "Yes, I do still want the store. You surprised me by your news, that's all."

"I guess I shouldn't have acted on Spence's word, but—well, it's Spence. He wouldn't tell me something that wasn't true, so I assumed—"

"It's all right, Mac. I understand," she assured him.

"Are you still feeling bad?" Spence asked. She didn't sound right to him.

"I'm fine."

Before she could say anything else, Lucy arrived at their table with three glasses of soda.

She beamed at them. "Well, I guess I don't have to ask again who sent you those flowers, Melanie," she said. "It must'a been Spence."

Spence didn't hesitate to take credit for the roses. "Yeah, it was me, Lucy. Better not be anyone else sending Melanie roses or I'll want to know about it." He grinned at the older lady, pleased with himself.

"I'll keep an eye on her for you," Lucy promised with a chuckle, then returned to her post behind the counter.

Melanie glared at him. "How could you?" she demanded, anguish in her voice.

Mac burst out laughing.

Both Spence and Melanie stared at Mac in surprise.

"Sorry," he said, holding up a hand as he tried to bring his laughter under control.

"What's so funny?" Spence demanded.

"Melanie's the first woman I've met who complains about receiving long-stemmed roses. You're going to have an inexpensive marriage if she gets upset if you *spend* money on her."

Melanie felt very small. Mac was right. She was being ridiculous. "Spence, I'm sorry. I'd thought we'd—that is, I'm not comfortable being the center of attention." She peeked a look at him and was grateful he didn't appear to be upset. "The roses really are lovely."

He gave her an apologetic grin that had her longing to kiss him. "I would've sent them to your apartment, but you're never there."

"I know," she agreed with a sigh.

"Why don't you give your notice to Jerry? You can—"

There he goes again, she thought. Like a whirlwind, he was ready to rearrange her life before they'd even worked everything out. "Spence, we haven't discussed the, um, details yet. Don't you think that would be a good idea?"

"And when are we going to do that? You're working two jobs."

"I know but—"

"When will you have time to work on your new store?" Mac asked.

She felt her head spinning. So much was changing in her life. She needed time to think.

"And since we're getting married in three days," Spence added, "you have a lot to do."

"Three days?"

Chapter Ten

Spence stared at her. "Well, yeah. I thought we'd go ahead and—that's the fastest—"

He bent over as she let her head fall, hiding her expression. "Honey, last night we agreed."

"I know," she said with a sigh, raising her chin. "Somehow, it just hadn't computed in my head that we'd—that the wedding would be that soon."

"I figure Thursday night. That's why you need to cut back some of your working time. You've got things to do. Like talk to my parents."

He almost laughed at the panic that filled her eyes. "No, Melanie, quit worrying. They're going to be happy."

Mac laughed. "Ecstatic is more like it."

She still looked doubtful, but not as worried.

"You'll see, honey, it will work out."

With a sigh, she said, "You're right, Spence. I need to give notice. It's just that everything is happening so quickly, I haven't had time to think about it."

He hugged her close, dropping a kiss on her forehead. "I know, honey."

Melanie wanted to hide under the table. She didn't want to face Mrs. Hauk. She'd told the woman she had no intention of marrying her son.

"But...but I have to work."

"You said you were going to turn in your notice."

She'd forgotten she'd just said that. Was she going crazy, or was life flying by too quickly? "Oh, yes, but that doesn't mean I can walk out. It would be unfair to leave Jerry without help."

Mac slid from the booth. "I'll go talk to Jerry on your behalf while you rest and work out the details with Spence."

She'd barely given a nod, in addition to Spence's grateful smile, before Mac walked off.

"I—I feel like I'm in a whirlpool," she muttered.

"Sorry, honey, but now that we've made the decision, it's best to get on with it."

"I know but—I'm embarrassed to face your mother."

"I explained why she said that."

"But...how can I convince her that what you told her isn't true?" Melanie asked, nibbling on her bottom lip in worry.

"Now, don't get upset. Your stomach can't take it," he said, his hand massaging her right shoulder. "I gather it was a rough morning."

She nodded, not wanting to talk about the time

spent in the bathroom before she came to work. Instead, she took another sip of soda.

Mac reappeared and slid into the booth again. "Good news. Jerry called a part-timer who's been asking for more time. She'll be here in an hour."

Another part of her life whizzing by. She'd worked at the drugstore for three years. Now it was gone.

"He said if you need to, you can leave now, but it would be nice if you could cover things until she gets here," Mac added.

"Of course I'll stay. Let me out, Spence, so I can finish stocking." She bumped her body into his, expecting him to move, but he didn't. And a shiver ran through her at the contact.

"If you want to stay until she comes, you can wait on customers, if any come in. But leave the stocking to the newcomer."

"Spence, I can't do that. It wouldn't be fair. Jerry is paying me for—"

"Tear up your time card. Then you won't feel guilty."

A sense of relief filled her as she considered Spence's recommendation. She almost laughed out loud at that word. More like an order. But he was right. "I guess I will." She smiled at Spence. Her husband-to-be. Panic filled her again, and she took another sip of soda.

"You okay?" Spence asked.

She nodded.

"Well," Mac said, "I'd best return to my office. The Poindexters are coming at four, if you can make it. If not, you can sign the papers later. I'll collect the keys for you."

"Thank you, Mac. I'll be there." She looked at Spence, and he nodded. She'd always been so independent. In one short day she'd reached the point where she had to check with Spence? She shook her head.

Mac stood. "You coming, Spence?"

"Nope. I'm staying here with Melanie. When she's free to leave, we'll go over to Mom and Dad's, then apply for the marriage license, and all hell will break loose as we plan a wedding in three days."

"Let me know what I can do. You know I'll be there for you." Mac clapped Spence on the shoulder.

"Thanks, pal," Spence said quietly, gratitude in his eyes.

Melanie was jealous of the friendship Spence shared with his three boyhood friends. But then she remembered Jessica. The two of them were building a friendship that could rival the men's.

Mac walked away and Spence didn't say anything. Melanie leaned back against the booth, forgetting that Spence's arm was there.

He curled it around her again. She eased against his warmth, even as she warned herself not to get too comfortable. There was no guarantee it would last.

EDITH HAD RUN to the post office to buy stamps and mail some bills. When she came back into the house, Joe was waiting for her.

"Spence called while you were gone," he said, trying to sound casual.

But Edith knew her husband well. "What's wrong?"

"Now, I didn't say anything was wrong," he immediately said, watching her carefully.

She sighed. "Okay. What happened?"

"Spence is planning on visiting us in a little while. He wanted to be sure we'd both be here."

"Did he say why?" she asked, her heart beating a little faster.

"No, but Melanie is going to be with him."

"Oh, dear."

"Edie, I want you to remain calm. If those two are going to get married, I want you to remember the young lady is going to be part of our family, maybe the mother of our grandchildren. We don't want to offend her."

"No, of course not. I just wish—"

The doorbell rang.

She turned and hurried to the front of the house, Joe on her heels, to greet Spence and Melanie.

"Hi, Mom, Dad. You remember Melanie, don't you?"

Edith tried to smile warmly at the young lady. Joe was right. She didn't want to start off on the wrong foot. "Of course. Come in. May I offer you a glass of iced tea?"

"That would be nice," Melanie said, then added, "But could we sit in the kitchen? I'm not a formal person."

"Of course. This way."

Once they were settled at the kitchen table with their drinks, Spence cleared his throat. "We're here to tell you we're getting married."

Joe grinned and extended his hand to his son. "We expected as much. Congratulations, boy. You sure picked out a pretty bride."

Edith avoided Melanie's eyes, but she said, "Welcome to the family, Melanie."

"Thank you, Mrs. Hauk, Mr. Hauk."

Joe said, "We're not formal, either, Melanie. Call us Edith and Joe, or Grandma and Grandpa, when it's appropriate."

Edith watched as Melanie's cheeks flamed. Was she embarrassed that she might one day have a child? Or did she have no plans for children? "You do want children, don't you, Melanie?" She hadn't meant for her voice to sound so sharp, but she waited anxiously for Melanie's response.

"Yes, I do, but—"

"Mel's starting her own business, Mom, so we may put off a family for a while."

Though disappointment filled Edith, she was also interested in the idea of her daughter-in-law starting her own business. "Like Jessica?"

Melanie gave her first relaxed smile. "It won't make the money Jessica makes, and it's not food. I want to open a consignment shop where the Resale Shop is now."

"The Resale Shop? Oh, dear," Edith said, thinking of that dusty, dull store.

"I promise it won't look like the resale shop when I'm finished. I have a lot of ideas."

"Yes, of course. And I'll be glad to help you."

"More importantly, have you two set a date, yet?" Joe asked, and Edith couldn't believe she'd forgotten to ask that question.

"Thursday."

Edith and Joe stared at him, waiting for a date. She suddenly realized he meant *this* Thursday. "You can't mean—this Thursday? Three days? That's impossible! You can't do that, Spence. Melanie, surely *you*—"

"Mom," Spence said softly, stopping her. "We're going to get married this Thursday, with or without all the trappings. I hope you'll help us make it nice, but either way, we're getting married."

AFTER EDITH RECOVERED from her shock, Melanie decided the planning would go smoother if the women handled it. And it would give her a chance to talk to Edith alone.

"Edith, do you mind if we send the men somewhere and do the planning alone?" She finally got up the nerve to ask after Joe distracted them with talk about the four boys vowing never to marry when they were younger.

For the first time, Edith smiled at her without reservations. "I think that's a great idea. You two go somewhere. I know, take your tux to the cleaners," she told her son. "We'll plan the wedding."

Spence frowned. "Are you sure, Mel?"

"I'm sure. We have a lot to do."

He looked at his mother. "Don't let her do too much, or get upset. She wasn't feeling well earlier this morning."

Melanie glared at him. Great. Now she'd have to lie to Edith. Smiling, she said, "Just a touch of the flu or something."

Spence embarrassed her even more when he leaned over and kissed her. He took her by surprise and her lips clung to his until she remembered his mother was watching. She pulled away abruptly, her cheeks red. "Spence, your parents!" she protested.

"I'll take care of her," Edith promised. "You two come back for lunch. I'm going to put on a stew."

Once the men left the house, Melanie went straight to the subject uppermost in her head. "I know Spence told you I was in love with someone else. I wanted to be in love, and I fixed on…that man because…because I believed he would make a good husband. But it was a crush that disappeared as soon as I realized how things were with Jessica."

"I see," Edith responded, watching her closely.

"I—I…your son is special."

"I know, but do you love him?"

Melanie was glad she had a clear conscience, even if it did mean her heart would probably be broken. "Yes," she whispered. "I didn't intend to, but he's so sweet, I can't help myself."

"Good," Edith said, beaming at her. "Then let's get this wedding planned. Now, the three important parts are flowers, cake and music. Oh, and your dress."

Melanie waited while Edith paused, a faraway look on her face. Then she turned back to Melanie. "You know, you're about the same size I was when Joe and I got married. That may be hard to believe, 'cause I've put on a few pounds but—have you chosen your wedding gown?"

"No. Spence insisted on Thursday just this morning. I haven't worked out anything."

"Come with me." Without any more explanation, Edith got up and headed for her bedroom.

A few minutes later Melanie held up the ivory wedding gown to her and looked in the mirror. "Oh, it's beautiful. This was yours?"

"Actually, it was my mother's, but I wore it when Joe and I got married. I'd be pleased if you wanted to wear it."

"If it fits, I'd love to wear it," she whispered, awed by the tradition Edith was offering. "And if we have a little girl, she can wear it, too."

"Let's try it on," Edith said, her smile warm.

By the time the men arrived for lunch, Edith and

Melanie had made a lot of progress. They'd begged Mickey to put together some flower arrangements. The church had been secured; the local baker was already working on the wedding cake; and Florence Gibbons, the best soprano in the area, had agreed to sing.

Mabel Baxter was printing a program and helping Jessica, Melanie's matron of honor, find a dress. Ruth Langford was determined to give Spence and Melanie a shower tomorrow night at her house.

Just as the men walked in the back door, Edith exclaimed, "Oh, my heavens! We forgot!"

"What did you forget?" Spence asked as he headed straight for Melanie. He pulled her up into his arms and kissed her soundly.

She could get used to that kind of greeting, she thought hazily as she snuggled against his hard body. But the pleasure she was experiencing took a back seat when Edith explained.

"We forgot about your family, dear."

Melanie didn't want to discuss her family. It was different from the Hauks. Different from the warmth and support she'd been receiving the past few hours. Edith wasn't going to be as happy about the marriage when she met Melanie's mother.

"Um, it's just my mother. I'll call her this evening."

"We'll be happy to have her stay here with us. It will give us a chance to get to know her. After all, we'll all be family," Edith said, making a note on their growing list. "Does she live far away? Joe can meet her at the airport and—"

"No! No, she lives in Lubbock. And she won't need to stay overnight. I'm not even sure she'll come."

Melanie knew she'd shocked Edith. Her future mother-in-law stared at her, her mouth open. Melanie turned to Spence for help. "Spence?"

Since he still held her in his arms, he stroked her back, a soothing motion that helped. "Close your mouth, Mom, or you'll catch some flies. Melanie's mom isn't like you."

"Well, of course not, but...but she'll want to see her daughter married, surely," Edith protested.

"I'll call her," Melanie promised, though she dreaded doing so.

MELANIE EXCUSED HERSELF, leaving Spence time to talk to his mother without his fiancée hearing.

"You and Mel seem to be getting along. I thought you were unhappy about me and Mel marrying," Spence said, watching his mother.

"Melanie is a wonderful child. I'm delighted with your marriage." She put the lid back on the stew and turned to face her son. "Though I'd like you to go ahead and start your family."

Joe walked over and kissed her cheek. "That's my Edie. I knew you'd come through."

"Mom, we are not having a baby so you can win

that stupid contest,'' Spence protested, ignoring his
father.

''I didn't say anything about a contest,'' Edith
said, her eyes rounded in innocence.

''Never mind. I'd better check on Melanie,''
Spence said, turning toward the door.

''You be sweet to her,'' Edith warned.

Spence was trying to figure out how Melanie had
brought her mother around, when Melanie came out
of the bathroom. He met her in the hall, away from
his parents. ''Are you all right?''

''I'm fine,'' she assured him.

''By the way, do you own a pair of jeans?''

''Yes. I don't wear them very often, but I have
some.''

''How about boots?''

She shook her head. ''Surely you don't want me
to wear boots to the wedding?''

''Nope. But you're going to be a rancher's wife.
You'll need boots.''

''Am I going to have to help with all those cows?
I don't know anything about cows,'' she said, her
eyes widening.

Spence chuckled. ''Honey, you're so cute the
cows will just follow you around.'' He pulled her
into his arms again, pleased when she didn't hesitate
to slide her arms around his neck. ''But I won't make
you chase cows. You'll be too busy with your store
and—our other project. You didn't tell Mom, did
you?''

"Of course not. We decided to wait, remember?"

"Oh, yeah, I remember. The four of us are going to be in the doghouse when we finally do come clean."

"Children?" Edith called. "Come to dinner!"

Spence pulled Melanie with him into the kitchen. "We're here, Mom."

"Good. Melanie, would you get the napkins from the pantry?"

"Of course," Melanie agreed, pleased to be put to work. It only reenforced Edith's acceptance of her.

"Thank you, dear. Joe, you and Spence get the drinks and take your seats." She carried a large pot of fragrant stew to the table, then added a tossed salad and a basket of hot rolls.

Then she watched Melanie as she put around the napkins. "My, I never knew having a daughter could be such fun."

Melanie looked up, stunned, and then a beautiful smile filled her face. "Thank you, Edith. That's the nicest thing you could say."

Chapter Eleven

"What did I say?" Edith asked, puzzled, staring at Melanie.

Spence watched his bride-to-be blush and look away. Frowning, he got to his feet and wrapped an arm around her shoulders.

Melanie turned and buried her face in Spence's shirt, much to his surprise.

"Melanie, did I offend you?" Edith asked, her voice quivering.

Melanie shook her head no, raising her face to smile again at his mother. "Of course not. I—I didn't want you to know, but I don't really have a family. And it meant so much to me to have you include me in your family."

Edith and Joe both stepped closer and Spence knew his future wife had captured both of them.

"What do you mean?" Edith asked.

"My mother and I don't have anything to do with each other and...and I've wished for a family like yours most of my life. I thought, once you knew about my background, you would think I wasn't good enough for Spence and—''

Somehow the four of them ended up in a group hug, as both his parents interrupted Melanie with protests.

"Of course you're good enough," Edith said.

"Of course you're part of our family," Joe insisted.

The glint of tears appeared in Melanie's blue eyes, and Spence wished he was hugging her alone. In his opinion, they were having too much family right now. But he could tell Melanie didn't feel that way.

"I don't think you can be blamed for your mother's behavior, honey, so let's forget all about your past," he told her, dropping a kiss on her soft lips. Yeah, he definitely wished they were alone.

Joe pulled away, surreptitiously wiping an eye himself. "Here now, Edie's stew is all ready, and you're going to need to eat to get through the next three days," Joe said. "If you don't look healthy on your wedding day, the entire town will either think Spence is being mean to you, or that you've already started your family." He grinned and Spence managed a weak grin in return.

"Come on, Mel, let's eat before the stew gets cold."

The four of them sat and enjoyed a family meal, something Spence had always taken for granted. Somehow today, with Melanie beside him, he found an even greater appreciation for family.

MELANIE, after a real family meal, one she enjoyed immensely, found herself yawning. Spence caught her in the act and grinned at her. Then he looked at his mother. "Do you and Melanie have everything under control?"

"Oh, yes. Ruth, Mabel and Florence are helping, too, of course. But everything's been started."

"Okay, then I'm taking Melanie to get our license and then back to her apartment and let her get some rest. She has to meet Mac and the Poindexters at four."

"Of course. Dear, you'd better do as Spence says. You're going to be very busy the next three days. Oh, Spence, Ruth is putting together a shower for tomorrow night. You'll need to find something else to do."

"I reckon he'll have his bachelor party," Joe said, winking at Melanie. "But don't you worry, Melanie. I'll ride herd on him."

"Thank you...I think," she said with a smile. She turned to Spence, willing to allow him to plan her afternoon because a nap sounded so wonderful. "I'll be ready as soon as I help Edith with the dishes."

"You're doing no such thing. Go do your errands and rest. I'll have the rest of the day to do these dishes."

Before Melanie knew it, she was back in Spence's truck, her life moving at a fast rate.

MELANIE AWOKE from her nap feeling guilty. Spence had given her so much. What was she giving in return? She'd trapped him into marriage. Just like her mother had warned. And in return, he'd shared his parents with her. Would share his home. Would even share his money if she'd let him.

Well, she wouldn't.

That, at least, she could do. She could pay her own way. She prepared for her meeting with the Poindexters with determination.

After greeting the elderly couple and Mac, she signed the papers and received the keys. The Poindexters then left, but Melanie waited until she and Mac were alone.

"Mac, can the agreement be broken if the Poindexters get upset?"

"What do you mean, Melanie? If they don't like your business?"

"That or—what if my marriage doesn't last? Could they break the agreement?"

Mac raised one eyebrow. "You're thinking Spence will let you get away?" Before she could answer, he continued. "No, they can't break the lease because of your marital status. There's no mention of that in the agreement. After all, you're not married now."

Relief filled her. "You're right. Thank you, Mac. Please send me the bill. You have my address."

Mac grinned. "Yeah, but I don't charge one of the guys legal fees, Melanie, and since you're marrying Spence, you fall into that category."

"But as you pointed out, I'm not married to Spence yet. I need to pay you for your services."

He seemed to be measuring her with his gaze. "Okay, I'll send you a bill."

"Thank you." She walked out of his office, the keys clutched in her hands. She wanted to go to the shop now, but she was supposed to start work at Jess's restaurant at four-thirty, only ten minutes away. Time for a quick peek.

She unlocked the door of the store and stepped into its shadowy depths. She'd dreamed of having her own business for years. Now it was coming true.

She jotted down a brief list of people to contact tomorrow. She'd need a good electrician, a painter, a carpenter. She'd need to advertise in the paper for people with things to sell. There was so much to be done.

After locking up, she hurried over to the restaurant, but her mind and her heart were still in the shop.

"What are you doing here?" Jessica asked as she came in the door.

Melanie came to an abrupt halt. "I start work in—" she looked at her watch "—two minutes. Why wouldn't I be here?"

"Spence stopped by earlier to tell me I'd need to replace you," Jessica said, her voice a little stiff.

Melanie stared at her with her mouth open.

"I mean, I know you have lots to do. But I thought you would've told me yourself," Jessica admitted.

Melanie felt anger rise in her. Spence. "I would've

thought so, too. But I didn't know Spence was going to do that. Have you already replaced me?''

''No. I'm filling in for tonight. But for the shower tomorrow night, I've called in an extra waitress to cover for both of us.''

Melanie took a deep breath. ''Jess, I need this job. I can't promise how long I'll keep it, but I can promise I'll give you notice when I have to leave.''

Jessica frowned. ''You'll keep the job after you're married? Mel, Spence has plenty of money. All four guys do. You won't have to work.''

''I pay my own way. I've saved for a long time for my business. But until it's up and running, I need some income. I quit my job at the drugstore so I could work in my shop, but I'll be free at night.''

Shrugging, Jessica agreed. ''Then I'll expect you here Friday night to— Oh! But your honeymoon. How long will you need for your honeymoon?''

Melanie's mind skittered away from the idea of a honeymoon. ''I won't be going on a honeymoon. I don't have time.''

''But Spence said—''

''Let me deal with Spence. We haven't discussed a honeymoon, but I'll explain that I can't.''

''If you change your mind,'' Jessica said with a smile, ''let me know and we'll arrange something.''

After that, everything settled into a routine that was soothing to Melanie. The sense of spinning out of control that had seized her earlier was kept at bay by the familiarity of the job.

Until Spence arrived.

"What are you doing?" he demanded.

With a sigh, Melanie said, "Spence, I think it would be nice if you greeted me as a normal person, instead of always coming in here and yelling at me."

"Okay," he agreed with a nod. Then pulled her into his arms and kissed her with incredible passion. When he finally released her, to the chuckles and applause of everyone around them, she was ready to kill him…or find the nearest bed. She finally managed to say, "That's not what I meant."

"Not good enough? I'll be glad to try again." He moved toward her, but she put out her hand to stop him even as she moved away.

"I have work to do, Spence. Go away."

"But I told Jessica you were quitting."

"I'm not quitting. We have several things to discuss. If you want to come over in the morning, we can—"

"You're not quitting?"

She shook her head no, then called the name of the next party to be seated. With menus in hand, she walked away from Spence.

When she returned to her station, she feared they'd have another argument. Instead Spence said, "May I pick you up in the morning for breakfast? Eight o'clock?"

She blinked several times, taking in his polite question, which countered the fierceness in his gaze. "Yes, of course."

He swept her into his arms again, his lips covering hers as he bent her over his arm, like one of those kisses in an old film. She thought she just might faint, like those old heroines, too. Because this man took her breath away.

AS HE DROVE INTO TOWN the next morning to pick up Melanie, Spence thought about his bride-to-be and their confrontation at the restaurant last night.

He still didn't understand why she would continue to work. Surely she understood he'd take care of her. He'd promised to do so. Probably it was connected with her shop. Maybe he hadn't made it clear that he would invest in it, that he'd be willing to give her enough operating funds.

He hoped that was it. Melanie was a curious mixture of warmth and generosity and rigid determination. He'd thought, after their time with his parents, everything would go smoothly.

He knocked on Melanie's door. When she swung it open, she appeared rested and happy.

"The crackers worked again?"

She nodded. "Yes, thank goodness."

"Okay, let's be on our way."

"I could fix breakfast here," she offered.

"Nope. Maria's just about got everything ready."

"Oh, no! I didn't mean to make extra work for Maria," she protested, concern on her face.

He took her arm before she could retreat into the apartment. "Lock up so we can go."

"But, Spence—"

He kissed her, something he'd wanted to do when he first saw her, but he'd been worried about upsetting her. "If we go back in your apartment, it's not the kitchen I'm going to."

She hurriedly locked her apartment door.

Once they were in the truck, she said again, "I thought we'd go to the drugstore or somewhere for a quick breakfast. I didn't intend—"

"You need to spend more time at the ranch, get used to your new home."

She chewed on her bottom lip, staring straight ahead.

"What's wrong, honey?"

"I—things are changing so quickly. I haven't thought about moving."

"I could line up some movers...if you want me to." He hadn't forgotten the lesson he'd learned last night. His soon-to-be wife didn't want him making decisions for her.

"No, it's silly to go through the expense of movers," she said, almost absentmindedly. "I don't have much."

"You might look around the house this morning and see where you want to put your things. Anything you don't think we need, you can sell in your shop. It would give you some inventory."

She stared at him in surprise.

"Or we can store it," he hurriedly added.

Turning, she looked out the window.

Spence was relieved when they reached the ranch. There had been little conversation the rest of the way. He felt as though he were tiptoeing through a mine field lately.

Maria greeted Melanie, warmly welcoming her to her new home.

"Thank you, Maria. I don't intend to change anything. I'm hoping you'll go on as you've been doing."

"Of course, Miss Rule. Whatever you wish."

"Please, call me Melanie."

"Thank you. Breakfast is ready."

Once they were seated at the dining table, rather than the kitchen, Spence tried to think of something to discuss while they ate. Something pleasant.

"Looks like spring might be coming early this year."

"Really? Why do you say that? It's still cold outside to me."

"One of the signs is the appearance of calves. Our first one was born last night."

Her eyes widened in excitement. "A baby? Can I see it?"

"Sure, as soon as you eat your breakfast. I'll drive you to the pasture."

"I can walk. There's no need—"

"It's a couple of miles away."

"Oh."

"You like your eggs scrambled?" he asked when he realized she hadn't eaten anything yet.

She immediately took a bite of egg, then buttered one of Maria's flaky biscuits. "Maria is certainly a good cook."

"Yeah. It helps me keep hands. They're not about to push away from Maria's table unless they have to."

"She cooks for all your workers?"

"I told you there's only four, and one of them is her husband. She likes to cook." Hell, Melanie was making him feel guilty for asking Maria to do anything. And he paid her a damn good salary.

Maria came through the swinging door, a plate of coffee cake and a pot of coffee in her hands. He'd told her Melanie didn't want coffee and he'd pass on it, too, but he hadn't actually forbidden coffee.

The aroma filled the room. The stricken look on Melanie's face told him that smell was having its usual effect on her stomach. Seconds later, she bolted for the bathroom.

He and Maria seemed frozen in their places. Finally Maria set down the plate and looked at Spence. "What is wrong?"

"Um, Melanie hates the smell of coffee in the mornings."

"Oh, I'm sorry, I didn't know—" Then she paused, a delighted smile breaking across her face. "When is the baby due?"

Chapter Twelve

"Damn it, Maria, no one is supposed to know!" Spence complained.

"No one? But they wouldn't be upset. Your mama and papa will be very happy."

"It's too hard to explain. Get some clear soda and crackers and I'll go check on Mel." He pushed away from the table. He was getting tired of this morning stuff. Poor Melanie must really be tired of it.

He met her in the hall as she returned to the dining room. "You okay?"

She nodded.

He started to warn her that Maria knew about the baby, but she pushed past him. Conversation hadn't been their strong point this morning.

Maria came back into the room from the kitchen with the crackers and soda just as Melanie reached her seat. "Here, this will help. It always did me."

Melanie's eyes widened and she looked at Spence. "You told her?"

"Nah. She guessed. Coffee affected her the same

way," Spence explained. "But, Maria, you mustn't tell anyone except Pedro. Mom and Dad don't know and we're not going to tell them until we have to."

Maria frowned but nodded. "You might try the coffee cake. Something a little sweet always helped me, too."

"Thank you, Maria." Melanie waited until Maria left the dining room. "I didn't know Maria had children. Do they live here, too?"

"Maria couldn't carry a baby to term. None of them survived."

"Oh, no," Melanie said with a gasp, her eyes filling with tears.

"Mel, honey, drink your soda," he urged. If he comforted her, he was afraid he'd take her upstairs. These close encounters were getting to be hard on his self-control.

She followed his direction as he cut her a slice of Maria's coffee cake. Nibbling on the cake, she seemed to be okay and he breathed a sigh of relief.

"How long will you keep being nauseous?"

"It's supposed to end after three months," Melanie said with a sigh.

"Hey, that's great. You should be feeling better about the time we get back from our honeymoon," he said, feeling a little better.

She suddenly stopped chewing. "I don't believe we've discussed a honeymoon."

"Well, I didn't have a lot of time, and that part of the marriage is the groom's responsibility. But I won't keep our destination a secret. I thought Hawaii would be nice." He sat back, waiting for her approval and appreciation.

She licked her lips and stared at her plate.

"Don't you think you'll like Hawaii?"

"I can't go."

He barely heard her, and her words didn't make sense. "What did you say?"

"I'm sorry if you're going to lose money, but you'll need to cancel the trip or go alone. I can't." Her voice was stronger now and she stared at him.

"Go alone? On my honeymoon?" He couldn't believe her outrageous suggestion.

She took another bite of coffee cake and said nothing.

"Melanie, what's going on?"

She sipped her soda before she answered. "I'm starting a new business, Spence. I have to be here."

"Your business can't wait until you come back from your honeymoon?"

She lay down her fork with a sigh. "I have a job, too."

"At the restaurant?"

She nodded.

"Melanie, did I tell you I'm willing to invest in your store? After all, we're—"

"No!"

Spence sighed now. "Honey, I haven't been married before, so I may do things wrong. I certainly have made a few wrong moves this week. But you gotta give me some help here. What's the problem?''

She didn't answer at once. Spence figured they were going to have the longest breakfast on record because he wasn't going to leave the table until they sorted things out.

Finally she said, ''Spence, I can't keep taking from you. I've debated breaking off the marriage, but…but my baby deserves the best. But you're giving me your name, your family…everything.''

''And you don't think you're giving me anything?''

She shook her head no, refusing to meet his gaze.

''Our marriage is just like any other. We share what we have with each other.''

''We're not going to have that kind of marriage,'' she said hurriedly.

''What kind of marriage?'' Although he was afraid he knew.

''A normal marriage. You said it wasn't necessary to…to do that.''

Spence was growing more and more depressed. Not only was he apparently not going to have a honeymoon, he wasn't going to have *anything!*

''I don't think I said that.'' Stupid, stupid, stupid, if he had. ''But, honey, we're getting along well, aren't we?''

''Yes, but we're not in love, Spence. You took pity on me at Cal's wedding, and now you're trapped.

I'm not going to force myself on you. Besides, I'm getting fat.''

Force herself on him? He almost burst out laughing. He was having a hard time keeping himself from chasing her around the table. "Mel, I've already told you—''

But she didn't wait for him to tell her he wanted her. "So I'm going to pay my own way,'' she continued. "I need to get my store working at a profit as soon as I can, and until I do, I'm going to continue to work at the restaurant.'' Then she took a quick look at him from under her lashes. "Anyway, even if I had the time, I can't afford a trip to Hawaii.''

"Let me get this straight,'' he said, finding their conversation difficult to believe. "You're not going to bed with me, so you're paying for everything.''

She nodded.

"Honey, that sounds like— Never mind. How are we going to have a real marriage?''

"You said it was all right if we didn't.''

He wished she wouldn't keep reminding him of his stupidity. "And I meant it. Sort of.''

"Sort of? Cal said you're a man of your word.''

"I am,'' he hurriedly said, thinking he was going to have to have a talk with Cal. "But since we'll be sharing a bedroom—''

She stared at him as if he'd said he'd murdered someone.

"Sharing a bedroom?''

"Well, honey, the minute my mother visits us,

she'll probably discover our sleeping arrangements. This used to be her house. Nothing is off limits to her.''

She swayed in her chair and he sped around the table to offer his support.

"I didn't realize— I thought we'd each have our own room.''

"Nope. And I don't know how long we can share a bed and not touch each other.'' He couldn't keep from smiling. ''My resistance is getting lower every day.''

THE SHOWER was overwhelming. The community was so generous with their gifts and best wishes. Melanie made sure Mrs. Myers was invited. Her friend across the hall hadn't made many friends because she didn't have a car or much income. Melanie was pleased when she was invited to join a bridge club.

But mostly, Melanie simply tried to cope. She'd interviewed an electrician today and he was drawing up a plan for her store. He promised to present it to her Monday.

The carpenter said he could work around the electrician. She'd scheduled a painter in two weeks. The only thing she hadn't done was pack.

When Spence arrived at the end of the shower, along with Cal, she remembered the biggest problem she had to face. Sharing a bedroom with him.

He was tender, sweet, considerate…and sexy as

hell. His strong arms made her feel safe, and more alive than she'd ever felt. His lips could be soft and gentle...or hard and demanding, and she was beginning to prefer their second role.

So how was she going to sleep in the same bed with him and not touch him?

"Ready to go home, honey?" he asked, bending to kiss her cheek.

"Are you two living together already?" one of the neighbors asked, her eyebrows rising.

Melanie gagged on the fruit punch she was drinking. Fortunately, Edith answered the question. "No, they're not. But it wouldn't matter if they were. They're in love and committed to each other."

"I didn't mean any harm," the lady hurriedly said. "He just said..."

"It was a matter of speech. I'm trying to be a patient man," Spence assured his audience with charm, "but she's a mighty tempting woman."

Melanie smiled, but she knew those words were going to come back to haunt them when her pregnancy became apparent. "I really should go. I still have a lot to do. But thank you all for your good wishes and all the lovely presents."

Cal helped Spence carry them to his truck. They practically filled the back. Then he helped Melanie into the cab. "Do you want these carried up to your apartment, or is it okay to take them out to the house?" he asked.

"Oh, the house, please. It would be silly to put

them in my apartment only to move them on Friday.''

''You're right. Why don't you come spend the night at the ranch tonight?''

''No, thank you. I need to do some laundry and at least start packing.'' She stared straight ahead, afraid he'd press her to come.

''Okay.'' He drove the few blocks to her apartment.

''There's no need to get out. I know it's late.''

''Melanie, honey, my mama always taught me to take a lady to her door. Besides, how else will I get a good-night kiss?''

Her body revved up with the thought of being in his arms. The climb up the stairs didn't raise her blood pressure nearly as much as the thought of his kiss. He didn't hesitate. As soon as they reached her door, he wrapped her in his arms and kissed the daylights out of her.

After several of those drugging kisses, he asked her again if she didn't want to come to the ranch.

''I—I can't,'' she said, practically panting.

''Tomorrow night, you won't have any excuses.''

''No. No, I won't.''

He kissed her one more time. ''I'll see you at the church,'' he muttered, his breathing as heavy as hers.

Then he was gone.

''EDITH, THANK YOU AGAIN for letting me wear this dress.''

Edith hugged her, careful not to damage the dress. "It looks wonderful on you."

Edith had taken charge of Melanie's wedding day, which was nice since her own mother already had plans for tonight and couldn't make it.

After sleeping in, something she hadn't done much of lately, Melanie had done some packing, mostly of her clothes and personal items. Edith had arrived at noon and taken her out for lunch. Then she'd insisted Melanie go to her beauty shop for a manicure, pedicure and hair-styling.

Next, she took her home with her and put her in a warm bath that almost relaxed Melanie. Almost.

Now they were at the church. Reality couldn't be avoided any longer. She was repeating her mother's sin. Forcing a man to marry her because of her baby.

She couldn't ask Spence's mother if she was making a mistake. But she badly needed reassurance. A knock on the door preceded Jessica's arrival in a beautiful green silk gown.

"Jessica, come in," Edith said, making room for Melanie's matron of honor.

"I thought I'd see if Melanie needed any help. Oh, and Joe wanted a word with you, Edith."

"Oh, mercy, what's the problem now?" She turned and kissed Melanie's cheek. "I'd better go check on Joe. He may have gotten into trouble."

"Thank you for everything, Edith," Melanie said, blinking rapidly to keep any tears from falling.

"It's been a pleasure, dear." Then she slipped from the room.

"You're getting a great mother-in-law," Jessica assured her, a smile on her lips.

"But I feel so guilty," Melanie protested, her agony in her words.

"About what?"

"Forcing Spence to marry me. I told him I could manage on my own, but he…he feels so responsible."

"So you don't love him?" Jessica asked gently.

Melanie couldn't look her in the eye. She sank onto the bench in front of the mirror, the old satin rustling as she moved.

"Melanie?"

"That doesn't matter. What matters is that he's only marrying me because of the baby."

"Is that the only reason you're marrying him?" Jessica probed.

"No, it's not. But that only makes things worse."

"Why?"

"Because it will hurt more when he…he gets tired of me and the baby." She finally raised her gaze to Jessica's, reflected in the mirror. "I'm afraid I'm doing the wrong thing."

"I think you're doing the right thing. Especially since you love him."

"I didn't say that!"

"No, you didn't, but you do."

Melanie closed her eyes. "I tried not to."

Jessica laughed. "Well, quit trying. It's okay to love your husband. In fact, it's glorious."

Melanie thought their situations were different. Everyone knew how much Cal adored Jessica.

As if she'd read her thoughts, Jessica said, "I haven't heard Spence protesting. In fact, he seems like a very eager groom, to me."

"It's time," Edith called in a loud whisper, sticking her head past the door. "Are you ready, dear?"

Melanie took a deep breath and stood. "Yes, Edith, I'm ready." For better or worse, she was committed to the marriage because it would be too embarrassing to end it now. She'd just have to be strong.

Edith gave her an endearing smile, a motherly smile, and Melanie almost fell to her knees. She'd have to find a way to make Spence happy, because he was giving her the world.

AS THE MUSIC CHANGED, Spence turned to watch for his bride. When she stepped through the church door and started down the aisle, he stopped breathing.

The bridal gown was old-fashioned but it seemed perfect for Melanie. Her cheeks were rosy red, like those of a shy young woman. Her gaze was modestly cast to the carpet on which she walked. Her hand was tucked into his father's arm.

With Cal standing beside him and Jessica on the other side of the preacher, Spence stepped forward to take Melanie's hand from Joe, eager to finally be able to claim her as his own.

Tuck and Mac were acting as the only ushers since there hadn't been time to plan a big wedding with more attendants. His two single friends had wished him well, though Spence could see they weren't as enthusiastic as Cal.

He nodded to the two of them as he took Melanie's hand in his. Then he turned to face the preacher.

"Dearly Beloved, we are gathered here to…"

Only a short time later, after he and Melanie had repeated their vows, the minister pronounced them man and wife and instructed Spence to kiss his bride.

His heart full, he lifted the veil, revealing Melanie in all her glory, and lowered his lips to hers. It should've been difficult to forget where they were, in front of a churchful of people, but he did. His arms encircled her, pressing her against him, his lips moved on hers, and he might've started seeking the nearest bed if the pastor hadn't interrupted.

"Congratulations, Mr. and Mrs. Hauk," he said after clearing his throat.

Spence raised his head, startled, then grinned sheepishly. His bride still seemed to be in a haze of sexual desire. He whispered, "Welcome home, Mrs. Hauk."

Her gaze sharpened, intensified, and she whispered, "Mr. Hauk."

Turning her around to face the crowd, Spence supported her with his arm. He could feel her trembling knees and hoped she made it through the rest of the evening.

The pastor introduced them as a married couple, then the music swelled and Spence and Melanie strode down the aisle, this time together.

The reception was at Jess's restaurant, of course, where at least half of their time, their battles, their discussions, had taken place. And where his wife still intended to work.

That bothered Spence, but he figured he'd fight that battle another day. He had more important things on his mind right now. Like tonight.

Even though it was a short walk, two blocks, to the restaurant, Spence had parked the car he'd purchased for Melanie, a Lexus, outside the church. He helped her into the passenger seat.

"Whose car is this?" she asked distractedly as he slid behind the wheel.

"Yours."

She stared at him in shock.

"I thought you'd need a car to drive, Mel."

"But this car is brand new."

Hoping to avoid another confrontation on the subject of money, he said, "I just never drive it. It'd get messed up driving it around the ranch."

Since they'd reached the restaurant, she said nothing else, and Spence counted it as a triumph. He led her inside. They were having the reception in the dance hall portion of the restaurant. When they passed through the dining room, however, everyone applauded.

"I think they're impressed with my beautiful

bride,'' he whispered in her ear. ''We should give them a show.'' Then he swept her into his arms and kissed her again. Those kisses were addictive.

Melanie blushed again, much to everyone's approval.

The band, waiting for their arrival, swung into an upbeat version of The Wedding March. Even though the wedding party and guests were only now arriving, Spence didn't hesitate to swing his bride onto the dance floor for their first dance.

Which is when he realized he never intended to let her go.

Chapter Thirteen

The rest of the evening passed in a blur for Melanie. She danced until she thought she would fall over. First Joe led her out as her surrogate father and new father-in-law. He and Edith claimed her as family. And she loved it.

Melanie enjoyed that dance. Joe, a non-theatening version of Spence, was wonderful. Then each of Spence's friends danced with her. She barely noticed whether it was Cal, Mac or Tuck. They were all fine men, but they weren't Spence.

It thrilled her to see Spence watching her from the sidelines. Though he danced with his mother, the rest of the time he kept his eye on her.

As she came off the dance floor with Tuck, Spence met her. "Time to cut the cake."

She hadn't even seen the cake. Edith had taken care of the arrangements, flirting with the baker shamelessly to get him to take the rush order. Spence led her to a beautifully decorated table against one wall. Its centerpiece was a three-tiered cake, with pastel roses and greenery decorating each level. She'd never seen anything so beautiful.

"It's too pretty to cut," she whispered to Spence.

Edith was already standing by to box up the top layer. "We'll freeze this and you can eat it on your first anniversary," she said. "It will still look as pretty then."

Spence picked up a knife. "Besides, if we don't share the cake, I'll have to fight everyone off with this knife."

He looked so dashing in his tux, Melanie thought he might be able to perform any task. Then he wrapped his arms around her, encouraging her to place her hands over his on the knife. They cut the first piece together and lifted it onto a saucer.

"Now you feed each other," Edith directed.

Spence got a gleam in his eye that worried Melanie. "Spence, you're not going to get it on my dress, are you?"

"Never, honey. You look too perfect to mess up. Now smile for the camera."

Melanie had scarcely noticed a photographer until that moment. She smiled at the camera, then turned toward Spence for the small piece of cake he offered. He popped it into her mouth with no mess, and she did the same with a slightly larger piece for him.

Then he kissed her, their passion blending with the sugar. "Hmm, I think this wedding cake is an aphrodisiac," Spence whispered. Then he kissed her again.

Still reeling from the passion that surged through her, she let Spence lead her back to the dance floor for a slow, romantic waltz while others lined up to get some cake.

Melanie couldn't imagine a more perfect wedding.

BY THE TIME they left the reception, Spence's body was tighter than a drum. Every time he touched Melanie, anticipation grew. And yet he told himself repeatedly that he would probably go to bed unsatisfied.

He'd given his word, and he was going to keep it...even if it killed him.

Their send-off was loud and happy, and they pulled away from the restaurant dragging a number of soda cans and balloons.

"I didn't know anyone decorated cars like this anymore," Melanie said, her eyes wide at the noise that accompanied them.

He grinned. "Yeah, you missed Cal and Jessica's send-off because—" Oops. Not a good subject. "Anyway, we decorated their car, too."

"I see."

He picked up her hand and held it against his thigh as he drove through the quiet town to their home. "You tired?"

"Yes. But it's been a lovely day. The wedding was beautiful."

"Not as beautiful as the bride," he said, raising her hand to his lips.

"Th-thank you."

"Do you want me to stop and strip off all the cans and things now, or can you stand it until we get home?"

"I don't mind. There's no one out here to even notice," she said just before a carful of teenagers raced by, blowing their horn in greeting. She chuckled. "Well, almost no one."

He loved the sound of her laughter. She almost seemed surprised every time she laughed.

"Tomorrow you can sleep in, can't you? You've already made arrangements for the contractors to talk to you Monday, haven't you?"

"Yes. But I have to decide what to do about the things in my apartment."

"Oh, I forgot. The guys all agreed to load everything up in our trucks on Saturday. It's still too cold to rodeo, and that will be better exercise than playing pool. So, rest tomorrow and we'll work on the apartment together on Saturday."

"I don't want to cause any trouble," she said, a frown on her face.

"Honey, you can't be independent when you've got furniture to move. You're not big enough to lift everything. Besides, it wouldn't be good for the baby."

They had reached the ranch house by then. He got her suitcase out of the trunk of the car, catching up with her as she reached the porch steps. The ivory satin of her gown shone in the moonlight and he thought she looked like a magical being. A perfect fairy.

"You're beautiful," he whispered. Setting her suitcase on the porch, he scooped her up into his arms.

"Spence!" she called, clutching his neck. "What are you doing?"

"Following tradition, Mrs. Hauk. I'm carrying my bride over the threshold." He maneuvered the doorknob and carried her into the house he'd lived in all his life. Maria had been on a two-day cleaning jag, though he'd assured her the house was perfect as it was.

"Oh," Melanie said, with a deep breath. Maria had left scented candles burning, the furniture gleaming in their light. Several flower arrangements had been ordered from Mickey so that the scent of fresh flowers filled the air. "It's beautiful."

"Yeah. I'll get your bag." He brought it in from the porch and ran it upstairs to the master bedroom. It, too, had fresh flowers and scented candles.

He came back downstairs to find his wife reading a note from Maria. "What's it say?"

"She left snacks in the refrigerator in case we forgot to eat anything at the reception. Isn't that sweet?" Melanie asked, raising her face to his, a beautiful smile on her lips.

He didn't point out that Maria got paid to provide food. He knew his cook's efforts went beyond what was required of her. They all considered each other family. But that was a new feeling to Melanie.

"So let's eat," he said before giving her a teasing kiss. He was hungry for more than food, but he figured he'd better take things slow and easy.

He just hoped "slow and easy" didn't mean years and years.

MELANIE ATE to please Spence. Anything to please Spence. He was so perfect. He'd undone his bow tie and opened several buttons on his tuxedo shirt, shedding his jacket onto the back of one of the chairs. He looked sophisticated and sexy.

And all male.

In the white shirt, his shoulders and chest appeared massive. Having recently been pressed against that particular area, Melanie could attest to his strength.

How was she going to resist him? And should she? The biggest reason to do so was to protect herself. She couldn't let him know how much she cared about him. It would make her more vulnerable.

But she wasn't sure she could deny him anything.

Because half the battle would be with herself. If he wanted her, whatever his reason, even if only for a while, she suddenly realized she wouldn't turn him down. At least, if he made love to her, she'd have those memories.

And she'd already promised herself she wouldn't be the bitter person her mother was.

Her gaze remained fixed on his masculine splendor, the food leaving no impression on her.

"Honey, if you don't stop staring at me like that, I'm going to beg you to let me take you upstairs and make love to you." He said it with a teasing laugh, a sparkle in his eyes, that set off fireworks in her.

"Okay," she said, smiling. She'd made her decision.

"Okay, you won't look at me like that anymore, or okay, I can carry you upstairs?" he questioned, his hazel eyes darkening.

"Whichever you want, but I'd prefer the second one." She held her breath, unsure what he would say. She only knew her decision felt so right. To spend her nights in Spence's arms was all she could ask.

He said nothing. But he began stacking the plates he'd pulled from the refrigerator back in it at precarious angles as fast as he could. Then, leaving everything else on the table, he lifted her from her chair and started for the stairs.

"The dishes! We should—"

"No, we shouldn't," he assured her. "We're newlyweds. We have more important priorities." He stopped at the bottom of the stairs and kissed her. When he lifted his mouth from hers, he said, "This is your last chance to stop me, honey. Speak now...and I'll die."

She tightened her hold around his neck and reached up to kiss him again. He got the message.

By the time he reached the top of the stairs, he

was breathing heavily, but that may have had something to do with Melanie's attempt to kiss his face and neck, or her hand trailing over his chest through his open shirt.

He set her on the edge of the bed and popped his tuxedo buttons in several directions as he yanked his shirt off.

"My dress," Melanie gasped. "It has all those thousands of buttons."

"Turn around. I'll undo them," he promised. When she turned her back to him, he couldn't believe the number of buttons. He hadn't noticed them before. "Damn! They sure wanted to make it hard on the groom, didn't they?"

"And the bride," she said huskily, which inspired Spence to hurry even more.

As the satin gown opened under his busy fingers, his lips trailed kisses down her back. Melanie wanted to return the favor. "Hurry, Spence."

When she could finally step out of the gown, he helped her dispose of her undergarments. More modern pieces, they were easily removed.

Though Melanie was self-conscious about her pregnancy, Spence seemed moved by the changes in her body, particularly caressing her small tummy where the first signs of their child were appearing.

"Oh, Spence," she crooned as he kissed her stomach, making her feel, for the first time, that the pregnancy wasn't a burden. Tears appeared in her eyes.

Maybe…maybe one day he would be happy about their family.

His mouth came back to hers, giving her those deep, drugging kisses, slanting his lips over hers, asking for her passion in return. She met him on every level, trying to touch all of him, to know him as intimately as possible.

Though Melanie had been divested of all her clothing, Spence still wore his briefs. When she tugged at them impatiently, he stripped them from his body and rejoined her on the bed. She reveled in his powerful strength as he pulled her against him.

"Melanie, I can't last much longer. I'm been dreaming of this moment since I held you at the church," he whispered before kissing her again.

"Then don't wait," she said with a gasp, thinking she would die if he waited any longer. When he plunged into her, she felt the connection to the very depths of her soul. She hadn't been able to explain it when it had happened the first time. She couldn't now.

But it was incredible.

And it only got better.

When they both went over the top and slumped against each other in exhaustion, Melanie finally believed she hadn't made a mistake, that she and Spence, along with their baby, could make a family.

He gathered her against him, his lips going to her neck, gently caressing. "I'm glad you changed your mind, honey."

Satisfied, sated, half-asleep, she murmured, "Yes, I am, too. I owed you so much I couldn't—"

All gentleness left him. He stiffened, pulling away from her. "You owed me? This...this lovemaking was payment?"

He'd misunderstood, she knew. And she could explain it all if she said she loved him. But she panicked. She couldn't pull herself together that quickly. All she did was stare at him in the candlelight.

He ripped himself from the bed. Standing in the shadows, like a giant staring down, he whispered, "You don't owe me anything, Melanie, most of all your body. Good night!"

And he left her there alone in their bed. Melanie hadn't wanted to risk her heart, but she wasn't willing to send Spence away. She got up and dug into her suitcase for her robe, but it took precious minutes to find it. After covering her naked body with it, she hurried down the stairs.

But Spence wasn't there.

She stared out the back door, unsure where he might've gone. Unfamiliar with the ranch, she didn't know where to look.

Finally she trudged back up the stairs to the lonely, empty bed. She propped herself up with pillows, determined to remain awake until he returned.

But sleep overcame her long before dawn.

WHEN MELANIE FINALLY did get to sleep, she didn't awaken until almost eleven o'clock the next morning.

For the next half hour, she tried to calm herself, to think of ways of making up with Spence. Until she heard footsteps pounding up the stairs.

But they weren't Spence's. Maria burst through the door. "Quick. Edith and Joe are here. You must get dressed and come down so they do not know you have morning sickness."

The next couple of minutes were frantic as Maria unzipped the suitcase and pulled out something for Melanie to wear and she dressed. After running a quick comb through her hair, ignoring her pale face, she hurried down the stairs after Maria.

"Good morning," Edith said as Melanie entered the kitchen. "I hope we're not here too early."

"Not at all. I'm glad you came. I was just upstairs settling in. We…we didn't do much unpacking last night."

Joe broke into laughter he tried to cover up when all three women looked at him. "Uh, no, it was kind of late."

Maria, after a look at Melanie, said, "Spence will be in for lunch shortly. Will you join us?"

"We don't want to intrude," Edith said.

"No, please, join us," Melanie urged. Better to see Spence first when other people were around. "I hadn't realized so much time had passed."

"I'm glad you're settling in so well," Edith said, beaming at her. "Do you want to show me what you've done?"

Melanie almost choked. She pictured the bedroom

as she'd left it, the bedcovers in total disarray, a suitcase open on the floor with its contents dumped out beside it. "Uh, no, I'm not ready yet. Maybe later. But you will stay to lunch, won't you?"

"'Course we will," Joe assured her. "We never pass up Maria's cooking."

After she led them to the kitchen and they all sat at the table, Maria put a cup of hot tea in front of her and Melanie relaxed against the back of the chair. She doctored the tea with cream and sugar and decided she was going to survive the roller-coaster ride her life was on.

Until Spence opened the back door.

They all turned, and Melanie watched as his gaze took in his parents. His expression, one of anger, turned to a guarded look as he greeted them.

"Mom, Dad, I didn't know you were coming."

"Well, we brought more gifts that were left at the wedding. Though maybe you two would want to open them today," Joe explained. "Though you look kind of tired, son."

"I didn't get much sleep last night," Spence said as he moved to the refrigerator.

Joe laughed again, and even Edith smirked at their son's response, putting a totally different meaning on his words than Melanie thought he meant. In fact, he shot her a hard look that his parents missed.

"That's not a surprise, boy," Joe said.

"Joe, behave yourself. The ladies invited us to

lunch. You don't mind, do you, dear?'' Edith asked her son.

"You're always welcome, Mom. How long until lunch, Maria?''

"Probably half an hour if you want a shower,'' his housekeeper answered.

"Good idea,'' he said, heading for the stairs.

"You go with him, Melanie, dear,'' Edith urged. "I'll help Maria.''

"And I'm walking out to the barn. Be back in a little while, Maria,'' Joe said, lumbering up from his chair and heading out the back door.

Melanie had no choice. She slowly climbed the stairs. By the time she reached the bedroom, Spence had already started his shower. She tidied up the bed and put her belongings back into the suitcase. Where she was sleeping that night was still a question mark. No point in unpacking until things were settled.

By the time Spence emerged from the bathroom, the room was immaculate, as Maria always left it. He opened the door, wrapped in a towel around his hips and nothing else.

Melanie was sitting primly on the side of the bed.

He looked around to be sure she was alone.

"What do you want?'' he asked harshly.

"Your mom insisted I come up with you.'' She didn't look at him after that first glance. The sight of his bare chest reminded her too much of the joy of last evening.

Before she opened her mouth and ruined everything.

"You straightened the bedroom."

She darted a quick look and then away. "I wouldn't have left it like that but…but I overslept and then Maria came running up to tell me they'd arrived and—"

"I see." He crossed the room to the large chest of drawers that stood against one wall. He took out clean briefs, jeans and socks. Then he removed a clean shirt from the closet.

As he crossed back in front of her, Melanie said, "About last night—"

"I don't have time for that," he said, his voice hard and disinterested. "Lunch will be ready before I can get dressed now."

As if lunch was more important than their marriage.

He closed the bathroom door behind him.

Melanie slumped on the bed. What should she do? He'd wanted sex, she knew that much. But he didn't love her. He hadn't told her so.

And he was so angry with her now, he'd sooner spit on her than kiss her.

The door opened again and he appeared fully dressed. "Are you coming?" he asked, walking by her.

She didn't answer, so he stopped at the door. "Well?"

"Yes, of course," she said, rising. It was all she

could do. To embarrass him by not playing hostess to his parents would only make matters worse.

"You can't go down like that," he protested as she walked toward the door.

She looked down at the denim dress she was wearing, wondering what was wrong. "Why not?"

"Because you look like you're going to someone's funeral."

Before she could put on a smile, he pulled her against him and dropped a hard kiss on her lips. Then he turned his back on her and went down the stairs.

"Spence—" she called, reaching for him, but her voice was barely a whisper and he didn't turn. But he should have heard her heart breaking.

Because he hadn't kissed her as he had last night. Warm, loving, caring. No, that had been a kiss of dismissal, of anger. And she mourned what she had lost.

Chpater Fourteen

Spence was mad.

But he couldn't let it show in front of his parents.

He couldn't believe his wedding night. The most incredible sex he'd ever had with the woman he loved. Because she owed him.

Yep, he was mad.

He hadn't been able to get to sleep. He'd paced out in the barn for hours. Then, at five, he'd made a pot of coffee and started work, trying to forget his wedding night. But with his parents' arrival, he had to face her, and that made forgetting even more difficult.

Over lunch, she'd talked to his parents, carried the conversation while he'd eaten, saying nothing. After receiving some stares from his parents, he made an effort. But lack of sleep was catching up with him. That and wanting Melanie.

Damn! He shouldn't want her. He shouldn't want any woman who offered herself because she *owed* him. But sex with Melanie, as it had been that first time, at Cal and Jessica's wedding, was beyond description. In addition to the physical pleasures, he'd felt a bonding of their souls, a melding of their minds, a oneness he'd never experienced before.

"Son?" his father said.

"Yeah?"

"I asked if you wanted to help me bring in the gifts. You acted like you didn't hear me."

He tried a grin. "Lack of sleep makes my ears weak."

"Then I predict a hearing problem for a long time," Joe teased, shifting his gaze to include Melanie.

Spence felt his face grow hot as his mother looked his way.

"What?" she asked. "Your ears are bothering you?"

"No, Mom. Dad was just teasing. We're going to bring in the presents you brought over."

"Oh, yes. Melanie, we'll need paper and pen to make a list," Edith said.

He knew Melanie had no idea where to find such items in his house. After all, he hadn't even given her a tour. All she'd seen was the kitchen and his bed. "In the desk in the den," he told her gruffly, pointing in the right direction. Then he followed his father from the house.

"You okay?" Joe asked as soon as they were out of the house.

"Yeah, but I need some sleep bad."

Joe chuckled. "Maybe the two of you can get some sleep tonight."

"Melanie's working tonight."

"What?" Joe asked in surprise.

"She kept her job at the restaurant. She wants to pay her own way." He could barely get out those last words, but his father didn't seem to notice.

"What a sweet child."

"I'm supposed to pay for things!" he snapped, and then regretted his response.

Joe stared at him and then burst into laughter again. "Is that what's bothering you, boy? That she wants to contribute to the family? Lord love you, go down on your knees and be grateful. A lot of women want to spend the money faster than you can make it."

"I know but—"

"I know we've got plenty of money, but you wouldn't want a woman who married you for the money."

"No." His father had warned him about women who would do anything to marry a meal ticket. He hadn't looked at it from that perspective. He'd thought it cute that Melanie was independent. Until she carried it to extremes.

"Now, come on. Let's get those presents."

The rest of the afternoon, they unwrapped presents and made notes of the givers. Edith teased Spence about helping Melanie write the thank-you notes. Joe spent his time wadding up the wrapping paper and handing either Melanie or Spence another package to open.

One of the gifts Melanie opened seemed to entrance her.

He peeked over her shoulders and found a pair of homemade wooden bookends with two pictures of him as a little boy shellacked onto the wood. One was of him hugging his dog, an English retriever he'd had when he was four. The other picture was of him and his three friends, all on horseback when they'd been about ten.

"Who gave us those?" he demanded.

"A Mister Barney Gonzales," she said, continuing to look at the pictures.

"Those are great pictures," Edith said, a dreamy smile on her lips. "And if you ever have a little boy, I suspect that's how he'll look. Hauks breed true. That's how Joe looked when he was little."

Spence watched as Melanie's gaze turned as dreamy as Edith's and one hand stole across her stomach. Afraid his mother and father might notice, he leaned over and kissed Melanie, taking her hand from her stomach as he did so.

She gave him a surprised look, then followed his gaze to her hand. She hadn't even realized the gesture she'd made, he realized.

"It's a very thoughtful gift," she said softly, letting her gaze return to the bookends.

"Yeah, Mr. Gonzales was my Boy Scout leader. He's a great guy."

She smiled at him, the first smile he'd received from her since he'd made love to her. Not that he'd invited any smiles. But he enjoyed it.

Maria, who'd come in and out during their unwrapping, reappeared at the den door. "Are you two staying for supper? I'm making enchiladas."

"Supper? My, I didn't realize it was almost four o'clock," Edith exclaimed. "No, thank you, Maria, but we've got to go home. Come on, Joe. Let's finish cleaning up. There's a special program on television I want to see this evening."

His parents left in a whirlwind fashion, and Spence found himself alone with his bride before he knew it. But not for long.

"I have to go dress for work," she murmured and ran up the stairs.

So he didn't have to worry about dealing with Melanie. She had other plans.

MELANIE APPRECIATED the luxurious comfort of her new car when she left the restaurant that evening. Friday and Saturday nights, she had to work until eleven. After her lack of sleep from the night before, she was dead on her feet when she was finally able to leave.

Spence hadn't come to the restaurant.

Not that she'd expected him to. His message was clear the entire day. He was angry. She wondered how he'd spent his evening.

She made the quick trip out of Cactus to his home.

Their home, sort of. She still felt like a visitor, in spite of Maria's friendliness.

When she reached the house, the porch light was burning, but the upstairs bedroom showed no light. Wearily, she dragged herself from the car and closed its door quietly. Spence had given her a key to the front door as he told her goodbye. She tiptoed across the porch and opened the locked door.

Closing it quietly behind her, she locked up, then turned off the outside light. She trudged into the kitchen, deciding a glass of milk might help her sleep.

Maria had left the kitchen sparkling, as usual. Melanie wondered how women managed who came in from working to face a messy kitchen. She was fortunate she didn't have housekeeping responsibilities with everything else she was trying to do.

If only she had a husband who loved her, who wanted her, life would be perfect.

After drinking the milk, she rinsed the glass and put it in the dishwasher. Then she tiptoed up the stairs, dreading every step.

When she pushed open the door to the master bedroom, she discovered the bed still made and no sign of her husband.

Had he gone out? Was he partying because his wife was gone? She felt silly even thinking such a thing. Leaving the door open, she went back out into the hall and opened the first door at the head of the stairs.

This room had probably been Spence's as a boy. By the light of the moon, pouring through the window, she saw some trophies on the bookshelf, a baseball glove over in one corner. And a large body asleep in the queen-size bed.

She quietly moved to his side, staring down at his closed eyes, listening to his deep breathing. Neither of them had gotten much sleep last night. But she wished he'd waited up for her. She wished—

Leaving the room, she closed the door noiselessly. Then she explored the other two doors opposite the master bedroom. One was a bath. The other was also a bedroom with a double bed, decorated in blue.

With a nod, she fetched her suitcase from the big bedroom and made herself at home in the guest bedroom. She wasn't going to drive her husband from his bed. If he didn't want her, she'd find somewhere else to sleep.

At the last minute she remembered to go down to the kitchen and bring up some crackers. She didn't want any more emergency trips to the bathroom in the morning.

Then she crawled into her lonely bed for some much needed sleep.

SPENCE HAD THOUGHT about waiting up for Melanie. He'd warned her to lock her doors when she left the restaurant. But not having slept at all the night before, his body gave out on him. So he took himself off to his old bedroom. He certainly wasn't going to force himself on his wife.

When he woke at five, his normal time, he immediately looked out the front window, relieved to see the Lexus in the front yard. After visiting the bathroom, he returned to his room and dressed in the clothes he'd gathered up last night.

Finally, he could wait no longer. He tiptoed to the master bedroom and opened the door. Last night, before he'd gone to bed, he'd put crackers on a plate beside the bed. He hoped his thoughtfulness would make up for yesterday.

But he guessed they hadn't made a difference. Because there was no one there. The bed hadn't been disturbed.

Was she sleeping on the couch downstairs? That would announce to Maria that they had problems. He decided to check the third bedroom before he went downstairs.

After opening the door, he sighed as he took in her still form. Her suitcase had been carried in and opened. She had crackers on the bedside table.

With a heavy heart, he closed the door and hurried downstairs to put on a pot of coffee.

MELANIE HAD FOUND an alarm clock in her new bedroom and she set it for eight o'clock. Though Cal would probably be up earlier, she knew she needed at least that much sleep after the night before.

When the alarm went off, she munched several

crackers before she gathered her clothing and headed to the hall bathroom for a quick shower.

When she had carefully made the bed and hidden her suitcase in the closet, Melanie checked the master bedroom to be sure it was tidy. Spence had used the shower and left his towel on the floor. She put it in the dirty laundry.

She checked the bedroom he'd used last night. Making up the bed, she made sure there was no trace of his overnight occupancy. Then she hurried downstairs.

"Good morning," Maria said with a smile. "Are you ready for some breakfast?"

"Yes, I think I am. Some fruit and toast would be good. And a cup of hot tea. But I can—"

"No, you sit down. You worked late last night. Why didn't you sleep later this morning?"

"We're going to clean out my apartment today. I thought we should get an early start. Unless Spence has something else to do. I forgot to check with him last night."

Maria smiled, as if she thought they'd had other things on their minds when Melanie got home last night.

"Spence didn't say anything this morning. He gulped his breakfast down almost as fast as I put it on the table."

"What time does he usually eat?" Melanie asked as Maria served her toast and a bowl of fruit.

"Well, he gets up around five and makes a pot of

coffee. Then he puts in a couple of hours' work and comes in around seven or seven-thirty for breakfast.''

''He puts in a long day.''

''That he does. They all do. It's not easy being a cowboy. But they're special men.'' Maria grinned at her. ''My Pedro has always made me happy.''

Melanie smiled but said nothing. The teakettle sounded, and Maria poured the boiling water into a teapot for Melanie's hot tea.

''I'm going to get spoiled very quickly, Maria. You mustn't wait on me too much. Why don't you join me?''

''Well, I'm ready for a break before I start cleaning house.'' She sat at the table with a glass of juice.

''I straightened everything upstairs, so you can skip it today.''

''You didn't have to do that,'' Maria protested.

''Yes, I did. And it didn't take long.''

''Maybe I'll do some baking today with the extra time. Are you working again this evening?''

''Yes. Monday night will be my only night off.''

Before Maria could comment, the back door opened and Spence ushered in some cold air.

''I think we're about to have another snowstorm,'' he said, but Melanie noticed he didn't look at her. ''Have you listened to the weather, Maria?''

''Yes. There's a storm heading this way, but they don't think it will get here until this afternoon.''

''Can we still move my belongings today?'' Melanie asked, wondering if her husband would continue to ignore her.

He gave her a sharp look, then walked past her to the phone. "I'll call the guys and see."

Melanie finished her breakfast while he talked to his friends. As she drank the last of her hot tea, he hung up the phone.

"They'll be there in an hour. Can you be ready by then?"

"I'll be ready in about five minutes. If you're not ready to go yet, I can drive myself." She wasn't going to hang on to him.

He stood with his hands on his hips, his eyebrows raised, and she had to look away. Or beg for him to kiss her.

"I'm ready."

"Thanks for breakfast, Maria," she said as she shoved back from the table.

"My pleasure. Maybe tomorrow you'll eat a little more."

"What did she have?"

Both women turned to look at him. Melanie couldn't believe he'd even asked, much less cared.

"I had fruit and toast, along with hot tea."

"No milk?"

"I drank a glass of milk before bed last night, and I had cream in my tea. I think that should be enough."

"Are you working at the restaurant today?" he asked.

"I talked to Jessica last night, and she's going to work the lunch crowd, but I'll go in at four."

His hands still cocked on his jeans-clad hips, he shook his head. "You're a stubborn woman, Melanie Hauk."

"You're a stubborn man, Spencer Hauk," she returned and swept past him to the stairs.

IT WAS A LONG DAY for Melanie. She spent the morning packing boxes while the four guys carried her furniture down the stairs and loaded it into their trucks. Several things she gave to Mrs. Myers, including her television. Spence had several much larger sets, so she didn't need her small one.

They all worked straight through lunch, though Cal asked her several times if she'd be all right. Spence just watched her, as if he thought she might faint dead away. Once he insisted she sit and rest. But he never touched her.

About two-thirty, after they'd loaded everything, they all went to the restaurant for a late lunch. The wind had sharpened considerably, Melanie realized as she wrapped her coat tighter around her when she stepped outside.

"Come on. I'm got the truck warmed up," Spence ordered.

"It's not far. We could walk."

"Get in the truck, Melanie. That coat isn't enough protection for you to be out in this."

She got in the truck.

After parking the truck in front of the restaurant, alongside the other trucks, all loaded with her belongings, Spence wrapped his arm around her to hurry her into the restaurant. It was the first time he'd touched her since they'd made love.

"Are you all packed?" Jessica asked as they rushed in.

"Yes, thanks to everyone's help," Melanie told her. "I didn't realize how much I had."

"I know what you mean," Jessica said with a laugh. "I still haven't figured out where to put it all. Or the other things I'm going to need," she added with a lowered voice and a special smile.

Melanie returned that smile, but it suddenly occurred to her that they'd need a nursery, too. Somehow she hadn't gotten that far in her plans.

When lunch was over, Melanie took the clothes she'd brought with her and changed in the rest room. She wasn't looking forward to her job. She was too tired. But she had to pay her way. The men were getting ready to leave when she came out.

"We'll go on out to the house and unload. There's a storage building we can load everything into unless there's some things you need in the house." Spence waited for her answer.

"The other two suitcases should go in the house. But, Spence, I just realized I don't have the car here. Can you run me out to pick it up?"

"There's not enough time. I'll be back to pick you up this evening."

"But that's so late. I can—"

"I'll be back," he told her, and surprised her by dropping a kiss on her lips. But when his friends teased him, she realized he'd kissed her because of their audience.

She watched him go, her heart in her eyes.

SPENCE FED HIS FRIENDS Maria's enchiladas after all their work. She'd also baked several pies that they eagerly demolished. Then they sat around for a while, talking as they used to.

After a heated discussion about the coming baseball season, Cal leaned back in his chair. "So, how's married life, Spence? You seem a little tired today."

Spence felt his cheeks warm. "It's fine."

"You get much sleep last night?" Tuck asked, pretending indifference to his answer.

"Not a lot." Let them think what they wanted. They'd never guess he'd spent most of his wedding night in the barn.

The other three men chuckled.

"Well," Mac said, grinning at Spence, "I'll have to admit you picked a pretty bride. If a man is crazy enough to get married, he should find a bride who'll, uh, satisfy him."

"Aw, she'll do more than that," Cal said. "Melanie's a nice lady."

"Hard to believe you and Spence are married," Tuck said, rubbing his chin. "When our moms made that stupid bet, I wouldn't have thought they'd have any success.''

"I think you two should consider taking a lady, too," said Cal. "You don't know what you're missing."

"Bliss, right, Spence?" Tuck questioned.

"Uh, yeah, right."

"Do I hear trouble in paradise?" Mac asked, leaning forward.

"No! No, but there's lots of adjustments to make. Toothpaste cap, things like that."

Cal grinned. "Hang in there, Spence. And remember, the lady's always right." Everyone but Spence laughed.

"Spence," Maria called from the door to the den, "I thought I should mention that the snow finally arrived."

All the men jumped up. "We'd better be on our way before you have a houseful of guests," Tuck said, smiling.

"Yeah, I think it's a little early in the marriage for Melanie to deal with all of us," Mac agreed.

"And I bet Jess closes the restaurant early," Cal said, leading the way to the door.

"I'll come, too. Maybe Melanie can come home early," Spence agreed, trying to sound eager. He would be eager if he knew he'd hold her in his arms. He was finding marriage a frustrating proposition. "I owe you, guys," he added.

"And we'll make you pay," Tuck promised.

He smiled, but as he drove his truck into town, he

thought about that exchange and the words his father spoke about Melanie's determination to work.

What was he going to do? How long could he live in the same house with her and not touch her?

About fifteen seconds if he had his choice.

The wet snow splatted on his windshield, and the ground was beginning to be covered, though the roads weren't messy yet. They didn't usually have snowstorms that collected much, but sometimes they were surprised.

When he reached the restaurant, as Cal had predicted, Jess had already shut down the kitchen. Melanie was helping set up for tomorrow as the last of the diners finished their meals.

''Jess, is it okay if I take Melanie on home?'' Spence called, instead of speaking to his wife.

''Sure. We're just about finished here,'' she assured him with a tired smile.

''I'm not leaving until Jess can, too,'' Melanie told him, her voice firm. ''It won't be much longer.''

He reluctantly nodded, and he respected Melanie's refusal to abandon her friend. He and Cal pitched in with the heavy work. Fifteen minutes later, they were turning out the lights and locking up. The snow had thickened during that short time.

''I think this is going to be a big storm,'' Cal predicted. ''You be careful driving,'' he warned Spence.

''You know I will be. I've got precious cargo aboard.''

He felt Melanie's sharp look, but he helped her in the truck cab without saying anything else.

He had to concentrate on his driving on the way home. Melanie rode silently beside him.

When they reached the house, he held on to her arm so she wouldn't slip. Once they were inside, he offered her some milk or hot tea.

She refused both. "I think I'll go on to bed, thank you. It's been a long day."

Without comment, he followed her up the stairs. But when she headed in the direction of the guest room, he took her arm. "You're sleeping with me tonight. I figure you owe me for the move today, and I'm of a mind to take payment. You got any objection?"

He tensed as she stared up at him. What would he do if she refused? What if she hated him for even suggesting that she occupy his bed tonight? What if—

"I do owe you," she said softly. With a slight smile that offered hope, she opened the door to the master bedroom.

He stared at the open doorway, rooted to the floor, unable to believe her calm acceptance.

She stuck her head past the door and looked at him. "Are you coming?"

Oh, yeah!

Chapter Fifteen

Melanie supposed Spence was up at his usual time since the bed was empty when she awoke, but she really didn't know. All she knew was that his demand had given her an easy way out of her predicament. With his demand, she was able to return to his bed without discussing his anger.

She looked at her watch. Almost eleven. Spence was going to think she was lazy. If it weren't for the snow, she'd already be at the restaurant. But before they left last evening, Jessica told her not to come unless she called her.

She snuggled under the cover, her hand straying to her side, where Spence had been. Last night, after his sudden demand that she sleep with him as payment, there had been no conversation. The magic of his touch had made capitulation easy...and incredibly pleasurable.

Should she go downstairs to see if he was angry this morning? He hadn't been angry last night. After the first few awkward moments, he'd loved her as he had the night before, making her feel loved, wanted, a part of him. How could he do that when he didn't love her?

She didn't know, but she wanted to share the intimacy of marriage with him, as long as it lasted. So how was she going to do that? Did she have to take something from him every day? Did she have to owe him?

A sudden thought struck her. She examined it from one side to the other, looking for flaws. Would he fall for it? She didn't know, but she was going to give it a go. If it kept Spence in her bed, or more exactly, her in his bed, it would be worth it.

She reached over and picked up the bedside phone.

MELANIE TIDIED the upstairs again before coming down. She didn't intend to eat breakfast anyway. When she finally reached the kitchen, Maria was already preparing lunch.

"How are you feeling this morning?" the housekeeper asked.

"Fine. I'm sorry I slept so late."

"You're entitled. Do you want some breakfast?"

"No. I'll have a cup of hot tea and wait for lunch. Shall I set the table for everyone?"

"That would help. There'll be seven of us, unless you and Spence want your lunch in the dining room."

Melanie thought about that. Then she shook her

head, smiling at Maria. "I don't think so. How deep is the snow?"

"We got about six inches. But the temperature's down to eight degrees. It's really cold out there."

"Should the men be out there?"

"Spence has a stove in the barn, and he makes sure the men don't stay out too long at a time. Besides, since the sun came up, the temperature has risen to twenty-two."

"Ah. Balmy," Melanie agreed with a smile. "What are they doing?"

"Mostly they're making sure the water isn't frozen over, so the cows can drink. And any new babies and their mommas are brought to the barn. Sometimes they put out hay for extra feed."

"Spence said they already had their first spring calf the other day."

"Well, after lunch, you'll be able to see all the new ones in the corral on the other side of the barn."

Melanie hoped she could talk Spence into staying in this afternoon, but she wouldn't mind a visit to see the baby calves. She wanted to learn more about Spence's life.

"What else can I do to help?"

"Would you check on the bread in the oven?" Maria asked as she iced a chocolate cake.

Melanie was taking the bread out of the oven as the back door opened and the men hurried into the warmth. She smiled and nodded as each man introduced himself to her. She was glad to meet all of them, but she kept looking at the door. After the last introduction, she asked, "Where's Spence?"

"He'll be here in a minute. He was putting the last mother and baby in the corral and told us to come on in."

Maria ordered them all to be seated. She'd made a big pot of chili, its aroma filling the warm kitchen, cut up a large salad, added a bowl of corn, and Melanie put the hot rolls in a napkin-lined bowl.

"Is that chocolate cake?" her husband asked.

"Yes, but you get none until you eat your lunch." She looked at Melanie. "He likes his dessert first, but I try to reform him."

Melanie smiled but she thought she heard footsteps. Flying to the back door, she swung it open before Spence could reach for the knob. "Are you frozen?" she asked.

"Just frost-bitten," he assured her. His gaze stayed on her face, as if looking for something.

She smiled. "Lunch is ready."

"Thanks." He crossed to the kitchen sink and washed his hands before joining his men. Melanie slid into the chair next to him.

Conversation languished while everyone turned his attention to the hot food. Gradually, as they all warmed up and erased the sharp hunger, the men began to talk about their morning, sharing information about the condition of the pastures and animals.

Melanie listened with pleasure, seldom speaking.

Occasionally she caught her husband watching her, but she pretended to be perfectly at ease.

At one point, under his breath, he asked, "The chili doesn't bother your stomach?"

She shook her head no.

"You get enough sleep?" He watched as she flashed him a quick look before nodding her head. The vision of her curled up in his bed stirred him.

When everyone had finished, the men grabbed their outer wear and started back outside.

Melanie grabbed Spence's arm as he moved to join the others. "Spence? I wondered if you'd mind if I used your computer this afternoon?"

"You're not going into work?"

"Jess is keeping the restaurant closed today."

"I see. Yeah, feel free to use the computer. I'll be glad to show you how it works tonight, but I can't until then."

"It's okay. I know how to work one."

His eyebrow arced in surprise. "You do? I didn't see one when we moved you."

"I used one when I took some night classes."

"All right."

He glanced toward the door, where the last of his men were filing out, and Melanie thought he was leaving. Instead, he slipped his arm around her waist and hauled her against him for a long goodbye kiss that had her thinking of last night.

"I'll try to be in early," he whispered.

With that promise, he disappeared out the door.

She hadn't asked him about visiting the calves, but she could manage that on her own, she decided.

At least he wasn't mad at her. He hadn't ignored her. And he'd promised to come in early. That was more than she'd hoped for.

SPENCE HAD BEEN AFRAID to face Melanie. He felt guilty for insisting she sleep with him last night, but she hadn't objected. In fact, she'd seemed as eager as him once he took her in his arms.

But sometimes things looked different in the cold light of day. And it was certainly cold today. He entered the barn, the change of temperature welcome. As he walked down the center aisle, Cupcake nickered a welcome. He stopped to pat the old mare. "How are you, girl? Glad to be in the barn?"

He thought about Melanie patting the mare. He hoped he got to teach her to ride. He hoped she stayed that long. There was a real fear in his heart that she'd leave after she had the baby.

Somehow, he'd find a way to keep her. Her and his child. He needed both of them, but most of all, he needed Melanie.

He put in another four hours of work before he came back to the house. Maria had prepared dinner and left it to be heated up. She told him as they passed each other that she was feeding the other men at her house.

That meant he and Melanie would have the evening alone. He wondered if it would be awkward, if she'd talk to him or ignore him? If she'd come to his bed again?

The house was quiet. The warmth began to seep into his frozen body, but he wanted to know where Melanie was. Maybe she was taking a nap. He moved quietly into the hallway, preparing to climb the stairs when he heard the quiet click of computer keys.

"Melanie?" he called softly, stepping into the den. She was sitting at the computer, a stack of papers by her.

She jumped and spun around. "Oh! I didn't know it was so late. Are you all right?"

"I'm fine. A little cold. What are you doing?"

"Setting up files, doing a spreadsheet of probable costs, designing some forms I'll need."

He was impressed. "I didn't know you could do all that."

"I've taken a lot of business courses, preparing for the day I'd own my own business."

"I should've been taking those classes with you," he said ruefully.

"Why?"

"I own my own business, but I tend to shove the paperwork aside until my accountant yells at me."

"I enjoy it," she assured him with a smile. After a little hesitation, she said, "I could help you with the paperwork, if you wanted me to."

"I'd love it," he exclaimed fervently. Then he

paused. "I don't know, though. It might put me too much in your debt."

She dropped her gaze and he was afraid he'd said too much. Running her finger over the edge of the keyboard, she said, "I wanted to talk to you about that."

"About what?"

"Um, well, I don't think I can continue to work at the restaurant. It makes me too tired." She continued to keep her gaze on her fingers.

Spence almost stopped breathing. Where was she going with this?

"I wondered if…if you'd mind if I quit working for Jess."

"I told you I thought you should."

"It means I may have to let you pay for th-things for a while."

"No problem."

"It will put me more in your debt," she added in a low voice.

Feeling as if he was walking on slippery ice, he said slowly, "I think we can, uh, work it out, if you don't object."

"Okay."

Did she understand what she was suggesting? And why had she changed her mind? And wasn't he crazy to even be wondering when it meant she'd be in his bed every night?

"Okay," he agreed. "And you'll help me with the paperwork?"

"I'd like that. Why don't you show me what you need done?"

"Right now?" He'd envisioned some payback in the bedroom. He'd thought he'd hate the idea, but last night, Melanie had loved him as if her heart were involved.

"Are you hungry? I thought I'd work another hour, then heat up dinner. After you show me what you want me to do, you could go clean up, thaw out in a hot shower."

He couldn't argue with that plan, so he pulled out the disorganized pile of bills and paperwork. He was amazed at how quickly Melanie caught on to what he wanted. After fifteen minutes, he was free to enjoy his hot shower.

He went up the stairs filled with satisfaction. Not only had his wife indicated she wanted to be in his bed, but she also was taking a load of work he hated off his shoulders.

He knew which one was more important to him. He could do his own computer work even if he didn't like it. But he was discovering he couldn't do without Melanie in his bed, in his life.

AFTER A COZY DINNER where Melanie asked him lots of questions about his day and extracted a promise to take her to see the calves in the morning, they returned to the den.

"Uh, there's a basketball game on," Spence

noted, looking at her hopefully. "I don't suppose you're interested?"

"Not really," she told him with a smile, "but if you don't object, I'd like to look at some books I have. I could sit in here with you while you watch the game."

"Okay," he agreed, but he wasn't sure if their evening would work out. However, Melanie gathered several books on decorating and settled beside him on the sofa, next to a reading lamp. He sprawled out beside her, his feet, after he'd taken off his boots, on the coffee table, the remote control in his hands.

Two hours later he decided he liked sharing his evening with Melanie. When he'd gotten excited about something in the game, she'd look up and he'd explain. Occasionally, she even asked his opinion about some room arrangement. And all the time, her warmth was there, stirring him, making him anticipate the night to come.

He clicked off the television after the news that followed the game. "I'm ready for bed. How about you?"

"Yes. I can't seem to get enough sleep."

"I've heard of eating for two. Maybe you're sleeping for two."

"I guess so. I'm hoping to pick up a little weight this week before I have to see the doctor on Saturday."

"Since you're not working, you can get a lot of rest, make sure your blood pressure is down, too."

"I hope so. I'm going to have a glass of milk before I go up to bed. Do you want anything?"

"I might have another piece of cake."

As they stood, she slapped his flat stomach. "I don't know where you're putting it. It doesn't show."

"Hey, I work hard," he said, laughing.

"I know you do." Her gaze turned serious.

"So do you," he assured her, linking his arms around her. "And you're doing Mama duty, too."

She broke out of his hold, as if he'd made her nervous. "I'd better go get my milk. And I'll cut you a piece of cake."

He followed her into the kitchen, keeping his eye on her. Was she getting nervous about the unstated agreement they'd made?

He couldn't keep his hands off her as she opened the refrigerator. Pulling her against him, he nibbled on her soft neck, aching for her. Instead of protesting, she turned in his arms, leaving the milk on the shelf, and wrapped her arms around his neck. His lips claimed hers and he drank deeply of her magic.

When he lifted his lips, trying to be a reasonable man and not overwhelm his wife with his demands, he muttered, "You wanted some milk."

She lifted her face to his and kissed him several times, short, enticing kisses that lured him closer. "I'll drink an extra glass tomorrow."

It took him a couple of seconds to understand what she was telling him. When he understood she was giving him permission to forget their snack, he swept her into his arms and headed for the stairs.

MELANIE GOT UP to have breakfast with Spence when he came back to the house a little after seven. He was surprised to find her helping Maria put breakfast on the table.

"Are you feeling all right?" he hurriedly asked.

As an answer, she kissed him and then turned to pour three glasses of orange juice. "I'm fine."

"Why didn't you sleep in?"

"Because I felt too lazy. I have a lot to do." She gestured for him to sit. "Why don't the other men come to breakfast?"

"They fix their own breakfast at the bunkhouse. What do you have to do that's more important than you getting your rest?"

"Spence, I'm not an invalid. Besides, I may take a nap this afternoon."

"I approve," he said with a smile before starting to eat.

"May I come out and see the calves after breakfast?"

"Sure, as long as you bundle up. I'll have time to show them to you."

Melanie congratulated herself on her decision to quit her job at the restaurant. It had been a scary thing, to give up her job. She'd had a job since she was fourteen. She'd learned early she could only rely on herself.

But if relying on Spence, just a little, kept him at her side, it was worth it.

After breakfast, she put on her coat and mittens.

"Is that the warmest coat you have?"

"I'll be fine. I have on a sweater and jeans, too."

"We need to do some shopping for you. You need boots, too," he said, looking at her feet.

His offer to buy her things made her nervous. But she didn't want another argument. "We'll see," she said calmly. "Let's go see the babies."

He took her hand and led her outside. The coldness almost took her breath away. "I don't know how you stand it," she muttered, burying her chin in her coat collar.

"Maybe we should wait until it's warmed up," Spence suggested.

"No, I want to see them now. I'm fine. It's only for a few minutes."

He pulled her close against him, wrapping a warm arm around her, and she felt better already. They hurried to the corral on the other side of the barn, and Melanie climbed on the bottom rail. "They're so cute and little."

"They grow fast. Like all babies."

She looked at him and then away, wondering if he was talking about their own baby. A human baby was even more helpless than these babies. But she and Spence would be around to help her. Or him.

As if he read her mind, he hugged her close. "Our baby will be all right. Don't worry."

"How did you—"

"You always cradle your stomach when you're thinking about our baby."

She jerked her hand away and stared at the calves.

"Are you anxious for the baby to come?" he asked, his mouth near her ear.

"Yes. I—I want to get to know her."

"Or him," he added, laughter in his voice.

"Yes. Are you...do you—"

"Honey, I want to enjoy every minute of your pregnancy. I want to see your body change, our baby grow. But I'll admit I can't wait until our baby makes his appearance."

His eagerness was there in his voice, and it thrilled her. Afraid to show him how much she loved his enthusiasm, she looked for a distraction. "They look so cold," she said, pointing to the calves.

"Their hair isn't as thick as their mamas'."

"Will they be okay?"

"Maybe, if we're lucky. We've got the two newest ones in the barn with their mamas. And so far we don't have any orphans."

"Orphans? What do you do with them?"

"We bottle feed them if we have time. Sometimes we take them to the house and Maria tries to take care of them."

"I'll help her," Melanie said, her face lighting up. "I never had pets when I was younger. I'd love to help out."

"No pets? Not even a dog?"

She shook her head and said nothing else. After a minute, he pulled her from the fence into his arms. Turning her around, he kissed her, then hurried her back to the house. "Get warmed up and don't work too hard."

Then he hurried out to work.

Melanie watched him go. She'd enjoyed their visit to the corral. The more they shared, the more likely Spence would find her indispensable. She hoped.

After another cup of hot tea, she sat in front of the computer and began work.

At ten-thirty, she hurried into the kitchen to tell Maria she was going to town to meet the electrician.

"But the roads are still bad," Maria protested.

"There have been several cars going up and down the road, Maria. I'll be all right. And I need to get the work started on my shop."

"Does Spence know about your appointment?"

"Of course he does." She stepped forward and gave Maria a hug. "Don't worry. I'll be careful." She grabbed her coat and gloves and hurried out of the house.

SPENCE CAME IN for lunch, looking forward to seeing Melanie. It seemed the more time he spent with her, the more he hungered to have her close. He was already contemplating the evening they'd spend together.

He and the men all came in, cold and ready for a hot lunch. When he realized Melanie wasn't in the room, he turned to Maria. "Is Melanie working on the computer? Should I call her to lunch?"

"She's gone to town," Maria said, watching him. "She said you knew about her appointment."

"Damn! I'd forgotten." He moved to the window over the sink where he could see a portion of the road. "Silly woman. She should've canceled the appointment."

He was angry about her behavior. He didn't like worrying about her, feeling vulnerable. But there wasn't much he could do about it now.

"Shall we wait lunch on her?" Maria asked.

"No," he snapped. "We have work to do."

But he could hardly eat as he wondered if she was all right.

Halfway through lunch, the phone rang. Spence beat Maria to it.

"Is Ms. Rule there?"

That really irritated him.

"Mrs. Hauk isn't here at the moment. May I take a message?"

"This is Gil Bocker, the electrician. You tell her I can't wait no longer. I'm running a business. She can call me when she can get here on time!"

Spence couldn't speak. But the man's goodbye galvanized him. "Wait! Are you saying she didn't show for your appointment?"

"She sure as hell didn't. If she's changed her mind she should've told me."

"Man, she left here for her appointment at— Maria, when did Mel leave?"

"At ten-thirty."

That was over an hour ago. Surely it didn't take that long to get to town. His head started to pound; his heart to race. "Something's happened to her!"

Chapter Sixteen

"Cal, it's Spence. Mel left here over an hour ago to meet the electrician at the store and he just called. She hasn't shown. Have you heard anything?" After Cal said no, he continued, "I'm going to take my truck and head into town from here."

"Want some help, boss?" one of his men asked, but he told them no. He slammed out of the house as he pulled on his coat. His mind was racing with possibilities and prayers.

A little over five miles away, more than halfway to town, Spence saw the shiny silver Lexus sitting at an angle in the ditch beside the road. He could see Melanie's head through the window so he knew she was conscious.

He stood on his brakes, threw the gear into neutral and swung out of the truck almost at the same time. By the time he reached the car, Melanie was trying to push the door open.

"Honey, are you all right?" he demanded, yanking the door open and pulling her out.

"I'm f-frozen," she said. "I didn't know what to do. Your new car is ruined!" Tears ran down her cheeks.

"Who cares about the damned car. All that matters is that you're all right." He carried her back to his truck just as they heard sirens.

"That'll be Cal."

"You called Cal? Oh, that's terrible. He had to come all the way out here to—"

"To do his job," Spence assured her.

He slid her into the cab and cranked the heat on high. She was shaking, whether from shock or cold, he didn't know.

Cal leaped out of his Jeep and came to the truck. "Is she all right?"

"She's shaken. I'm going to take her in to Doc's."

"What happened? Did she slide off the road?"

"I don't know. I didn't ask."

Cal started toward the truck door.

"Not now, Cal," Spence protested.

"Just a question or two. I know how to do my job, Spence." He gave his friend a level look.

"Sorry," Cal said. "I've never— She's—"

"I understand."

Spence followed him as he opened the door to the cab, then stepped past him to put an arm around Melanie.

"Did you slide off the road, Melanie?" Cal asked.

"I tried to keep it on the road, but after that man hit me, I went into a spin and—"

"What man?" both men roared, and Melanie sank back against Spence's arm.

"A man in a pickup."

In spite of the terror filling him, Spence exchanged a smile with Cal. "Honey, could you be a little more specific? There's lots of men out here with trucks."

"It...it was a blue truck. He was going too fast and went into a spin. He came across the line and there wasn't anything I could do." She sobbed. "I'm sorry, Spence."

He put both arms around her. "I told you that car doesn't matter. You don't have anything to apologize for. Now, we're going to run into town and see Doc."

"I'm sure I don't need to. Really. I want to go home."

He silenced her with a kiss, stepped back and closed her door. "If you need to talk to her some more, can it wait until she's seen Doc?"

"Sure. And I will have to talk to her, Spence. Accidents happen, but leaving the scene of an accident makes that man a criminal."

"WELL, NOW," Doc said with a smile as he came into the examining room, but his sharp gaze was running over Melanie as she drooped in Spence's arms. "What did you do to yourself?"

"Nothing, Doc," Melanie said, her voice low. "I told Spence I was all right."

"You are. But your blood pressure is elevated, and

I think you might be suffering from shock. But you're going to be okay with some rest.''

''And the baby?'' Spence asked quietly.

Melanie's gaze stayed on Doc's face.

''We're going to check, but babies are pretty well insulated.'' The nurse came in, pushing the ultra-sound machine, as the doctor finished speaking. ''Lie down and let's have a look.''

She didn't want to move out of Spence's embrace. His warmth and concern had helped her. But she had no choice. She needed to know that her baby was safe.

''Looks like you're going to have some bruising from the seat belt, but I imagine things might have been worse without it,'' Doc commented as he parted the gown over her stomach.

''Will that hurt the baby?'' Spence asked, standing by Melanie's head, holding her hand.

''Nah. But Melanie will have a hard time standing up straight for a few days.''

Spence squeezed her hand.

Doc applied the jelly to her stomach for the sono-gram and then started checking the machine for a reading. Because of the bruising the pressure he was putting on her stomach hurt, but Melanie gritted her teeth and closed her eyes.

''You okay?'' Spence whispered.

She nodded, keeping her eyes closed.

''You've got an active little guy,'' Doc said ca-sually, his gaze on the screen.

"He's all right?" Spence asked hoarsely, and Melanie's gaze flew to the screen. Her child. She stared at the picture on the monitor, unable to believe her eyes. Spence's hand captured hers and squeezed. She looked at him, but his gaze was fixed on the screen, amazement on his face.

He loved his child. Whatever else happened, at this moment, she was thrilled to know that Spence loved their baby.

"Doin' fine," Doc answered. "His heart is ticking along just like it should. Want to know if it's a boy or a girl?" he asked.

"You can tell already?" Spence asked in surprise.

"Well, not for sure, but I'm getting pretty good at these things. Another month or two and we'll know for sure."

"Do we want to know, Mel?"

She appreciated his consulting her. She knew how anxious he was to have a son.

"If you want."

"We'll do what you want, honey."

She stared at him, unable to see any anxiety about the sex of their child. "Tell us, Doc."

"Well, I'd say you've got a little boy. A healthy little boy. And the nurse says you've gained three pounds, Melanie. Looks like you're doing well."

She smiled at him and then looked at Spence. He smiled, too, and bent and kissed her forehead.

"Now, Spence, I want you to take her home, give her a warm bath, then put her to bed. Tomorrow, you may get up for a little while, if you feel like it, but stay warm and don't do too much. I can't give you a painkiller and you're going to be uncomfortable for a couple of days.''

''It's all right. I'll be careful.''

''Good. And no more driving on icy roads.''

She almost protested, since her driving had been fine until the other car had hit her. But she didn't have to.

''Mel didn't mess up. A truck hit her and left her there.''

Doc frowned. ''Cal after him?''

''Yeah.''

''You take care of your wife. Leave that stuff to Cal.''

Melanie darted a look at her husband. It hadn't occurred to her that he would try to find the man who had hit her. ''No, of course not!'' she said anxiously.

''See? Her blood pressure will go up if you do.''

''I'll take care of my wife, Doc.''

Those words sounded like heaven to Melanie.

SPENCE WAS AS GOOD as his word.

He took Melanie home and carried her into the house and up the stairs, calling for Maria as he went. She hurried up after him, anxiously asking about Melanie.

After reassuring his housekeeper that Melanie and the baby were fine, he asked her to run a warm bath while he undressed Melanie. She protested that she was fine and could undress herself, but his gentle teasing about denying him the pleasure of doing so won her over.

Besides, the shock was wearing off. She felt stiff and sore and very tired.

After a few minutes in the bath, Spence carefully dried her off and helped dress her in a warm nightgown. Then he tucked her into bed and sat beside her.

"Maria is bringing you up some soup and a cup of hot tea. After that, try to take a nap."

She nodded, too exhausted to argue.

Maria entered with a tray. "Edith just called. She heard about the accident and wanted to make sure Melanie was okay. She offered to come out but I told her to stay off the streets."

"Good." Spence took the tray and placed it on the bed for Melanie. "Do you want me to feed you?" Feeling weak, Melanie indulged herself. "Yes."

Maria and Spence exchanged worried glances. Spence fed her while Maria hovered nearby. When she finished eating, Melanie scooted down under the covers, closed her eyes, and fell asleep.

"Is she really okay?" Maria asked.

"Doc said she was. He said she'd be stiff and uncomfortable for a few days, but he can't give her any painkillers because of the baby. The seat belt bruised her a lot."

"Oh, dear."

"Maria, I'm going back into town. Will you keep an eye on Mel? I'll take the cell phone with me in case you need me."

"Why are you going? The roads are still so icy."

"Someone knocked her off the road and left her there. I want to know who."

"Now, Spence, you should let Cal handle everything."

"She's *my* wife. *I'm* supposed to protect her. I'll be back as fast as I can."

SPENCE DROVE INTO TOWN, his hands clenched on the steering wheel. He almost lost Melanie and the baby today. And he'd never told her he loved her. He'd let her believe he'd married her because of the baby—because he thought she loved Cal. He hadn't wanted to be vulnerable.

And he almost lost her.

First he was going to find out who was responsible. Then he was going to beat the man up. After that, he was going home to tell Melanie how much he loved her.

When he entered the sheriff's office, there weren't too many people there. But Mac and Tuck were sitting in Cal's office while Cal talked on the phone.

"What are you guys doing here?" Spence asked.

"We heard about Melanie. Thought we'd offer to help look for the man who hit her," Mac said.

"Yeah, or help you beat him up," Tuck added.

Cal, hanging up the phone, said, "Hear now, there'll be none of that. You hear me, Spence?"

"Yeah, I hear you. Have you found him?"

"Maybe. Pete stopped a truck that may be him. Pete's bringing him in now." He stood and crossed the office to grab another chair from outside his office. "I assume you're waiting?"

"Yeah."

"Then sit down and behave yourself. How's Melanie?"

"Shaken up, bruised, but Doc says she's going to be okay. The baby, too."

"You got lucky today," Mac said.

"Yeah."

Silence fell, a silence filled with sympathy and support. Spence knew he'd been lucky in more than one way.

Cal caught a glimpse of the police car coming in. "They're here." As the other three men stood, he waved them back. "You stay here. I'm not having a brawl break out."

Spence followed Cal to the door, but he didn't go past it. Even though Cal was his friend, he was also the sheriff.

Pete, one of Cal's youngest officers, led a small, old man into the office. "Sheriff, this is Rudy Kato. He was driving a blue truck that had silver paint on it. He says he spun out on the road, but he didn't know he'd hit anyone."

"He's right, Officer," the old man said, his voice

shaking. "I wouldn't'a left if I'd known. But when I got the truck straighted up, I worked to keep it on the road and—I didn't know. He said I hit a pregnant lady. Is she okay?"

"Yeah, she's okay. But she may press charges, Mr. Kato." Cal's voice was firm and emotionless. "You were going pretty fast, weren't you?"

"Well, that icy stuff scares me and I was trying to get home. I didn't mean no harm."

"Go sit down over there with Pete and let him fill out an accident report," Cal ordered. He watched as the little old man trotted after his deputy. Then he turned around to face Spence.

"What do you want me to do? I can hold him because he did leave the scene of the accident. But I believe he didn't know he'd hit Melanie."

"Hell, I don't see how he even sees over the steering wheel," Tuck commented, staring at the little man.

Spence took off his Stetson and ran his hand through his hair. "I was furious, but it's hard to be angry when Mel's going to be all right, and...and he's so old."

Cal shrugged his shoulders. "I'll have the judge put him on probation and scare him good about driving dangerously. Will that satisfy you?"

"Yeah," Spence agreed with a sigh. "And thanks, Cal."

"You're a good man, Spence," Mac said, clapping him on his shoulder. "Forgiveness is a good thing."

The four men exchanged looks of a brotherhood that had lasted a lot of years and remained even after the changes in their lives.

Cal walked over to Spence. "You remember when I got shot?"

Spence's head snapped up. "Of course I remember."

"Well, events like today make you realize what's important in life. That's when I knew I was going to marry Jess. Because she was the most important person in the world to me. I guess you're lucky you've already married Melanie."

Spence was glad Cal didn't know what a fool he'd been. He'd go home and tell Melanie he loved her. It was time to risk everything. If he'd lost her—

"I'm going home to Melanie," Spence said, shaking his friends' hands and thanking them for being there for him.

"Good idea. Give her our love," Cal said, echoed by Tuck and Mac.

Driving back home, Spence realized he might even owe the old man a thanks. His endangerment of Melanie had brought Spence to his senses. He needed to be honest with his wife about his feelings for her. He'd realized that even without Cal's words.

He loved their baby. But he loved Melanie first and foremost, and it was about time he tell her.

When he got home, he wanted to talk to Melanie

at once, but she was still sleeping. In fact, she barely awoke long enough to eat a little dinner before she fell asleep again.

Spence made a quick call to Doc to confirm that all that sleep was normal and good for her before he took a hot shower and slid into bed beside her. Very carefully, he eased her body to his and slid an arm around her.

He wanted to hold her close, to know, even in his sleep, that she was with him.

FIVE O'CLOCK came and went the next morning, but Spence didn't move from the bed. After deciding that he was staying with Melanie for a while, he dozed off and on for several hours.

When Melanie stirred, then halted her movement with a gasp of pain, he came awake at once.

"Mel, are you okay?" he asked, stroking her cheek.

"I—I hurt."

"I know, honey, but it's the soreness Doc warned you about. How about I draw a bath for you?"

"Mmm, that sounds good, if you don't mind."

He slid out of bed as easily as he could, then pulled on some jeans and a shirt and headed for the bathroom.

After he'd filled the tub, he helped her to the bathroom.

There, she looked at him, frowning. "I'll need

help undressing and getting into the tub. Do you mind? I could call Maria if—''

"No, we don't need Maria. I'll help you." He helped her remove her gown and panties and hungered to touch her until she turned around. A wide bruise ran across the front of her body where the seat belt had been.

"Wow. I've got a tricolored wife. I'm impressed," he teased even as he winced at the sight.

"Really attractive, huh?"

"Amazingly beautiful," he whispered, and stood to wrap his arms around her.

She clung to him tightly, then stepped back with a sigh. "I need to tell you something."

"It can probably wait until after your bath. You'll feel a lot better after soaking."

She gave him an uncertain look, then agreed with a sigh. "Okay. After my bath."

He lowered her into the tub. "I'll go straighten up the bed for you." He hurried out of the bathroom. His libido could only stand so much time viewing his naked wife's body without reacting.

"Spence?"

"Coming, honey," he called, slipping into the bathroom to help her out and wrap her in a big towel.

"Here are some fresh clothes," he said, gesturing to a pile of clothes he'd gathered.

"Doc was certainly right about the pain," she said faintly as she leaned against him.

"You want me to call him and see if there isn't something you can take?"

"No! I don't want to do anything that could hurt the baby. I'll be all right."

After she dressed, he swept her gently into his arms and carried her back into the bedroom. He got her settled against the pillows again when she sighed with relief.

Turning to leave the bedroom, thinking she might be ready for some breakfast, Spence came to an abrupt halt when she said, "I really need to tell you something."

Spence sighed. He figured it was time for him to do some talking, too. He hoped he didn't upset her too much. "Okay. But I've got something to tell you, too."

Her eyes widened, as if she feared what he might have to say. "You do?"

"It's nothing bad. At least, I don't think— Never mind. What do you want to say?"

"I—I wanted you to make love to me. That's why I quit my job." She kept her gaze on the blanket he'd pulled over her.

"You did?" He was stunned. He'd thought she was trying to pay him back for what he'd given her. That's what she'd said. "Why did you want me to?"

She looked even more stricken.

He fell to his knees beside the bed. "Never mind. I have something to say, too. After yesterday, I didn't want to let another day go by without telling you. I fell in love with you last fall. But I knew you cared about Cal.''

Her cheeks burned bright red.

''I love you, Melanie. I have for a long time. I didn't want to tell you because of my pride. But now I have to tell you because I almost lost you. I love you and I always will. From now on I'm going to try to win your heart. But I want you here, beside me, for the rest of our lives.''

''Oh, Spence,'' she cried, reaching for him. ''I love you, too.''

He stared at her. ''You're sure? You're not just saying that?''

''I wasn't really in love with Cal. He just seemed safe. When you—when you touched me, I discovered that. I was so attracted to you, it scared me. Then you were so sweet, so gentle...so bossy, I couldn't help myself. I—we—I think we were meant to be.''

Slowly, gently, he lifted her against him and kissed her. Their ardor soon had them both frustrated. Spence wanted to celebrate their love in the most elemental of ways, but he didn't want to hurt her.

''Damn, we do get in the most awkward predicaments,'' he muttered as he lowered her back to the pillow. ''I mooned about the place when you wouldn't have anything to do with me after Cal's wedding.''

''I was embarrassed. And afraid I was going to trap you just like my mother had my father. I couldn't see you and risk you finding out about the baby.''

"Now I'm all you're going to see, Mrs. Hauk, for the next fifty or sixty years."

"No complaints here," she said with a smile, then leaned in for another kiss.

"If we don't stop this, I'll have to take a cold shower, and I don't want any more cold showers."

"Especially not when there's snow on the ground," she added with a chuckle that had her wincing.

"By the way, they caught the man who hit you."

"Who was it?"

"A little old guy, almost a hundred years old. Came about to my waist."

"So, I gather you didn't beat him up?"

"Nope. He didn't even realize he'd hit you. We can press charges if you want, but—"

"No," she said, caressing his cheek. "I'm so happy, I don't want anyone else to suffer."

"Me, neither," he whispered as he lowered his head for another kiss.

Noise in the hallway warned them of visitors just before someone knocked on the bedroom door.

Spence already figured out who had come, but he swung the door open for his parents anyway. Joe carried flowers and Edith some books and magazines.

"Darling girl, are you all right?" Edith asked.

"I'm fine. Just stiff and sore. Thank you for coming to see me."

"Of course we came," Joe boomed. "We're family."

Melanie smiled at Spence. "I'm so very lucky…to have my family."

Spence stood there smiling. So was he. So very lucky.

Epilogue

Edith smiled as she rearranged her cards.

"Wipe that smile off your face, Edith," Ruth warned. "You haven't won yet."

"Oh, Ruth, it's not the contest. After all, Melanie and Spence are going to wait to have a baby until she gets her store going. But they're so happy," she finished with a contented sigh.

Ruth muttered something under her breath.

Florence patted her hand. "I know how you feel, Ruth. I thought Mac would be easy to maneuver. I should've known better."

"You mustn't give up," Mabel encouraged. "After all, as Ruth pointed out, we don't have any grandbabies yet."

"Maybe they just haven't told you," Florence suggested.

"No," Edith said, her smile dimming a little. "I asked Maria if there were any changes, but she said no. And Maria would know."

"At least Tuck is showing interest in women, even

if it is in the plural,'' Ruth finally said. "I don't understand that boy. The other night he went out with Rebel Williams. She's been divorced twice and is no better than she should be. I don't want her for a daughter-in-law.''

"I'm going to have to devise a new plan for Mac. Maybe I can pay some woman to kidnap him, hold him hostage until she's pregnant,'' Florence joked, then narrowed her gaze. "Hmm, that's not a bad idea.''

"Florence!'' the other three women protested at once.

"Just kidding, just kidding,'' she said soothingly. "But the boy is frustrating me so much.''

"Oh, by the way,'' Edith said, excitement in her voice. "Tomorrow is the grand opening for Melanie's store. You've all got to come!''

"We wouldn't miss it,'' Ruth assured her, and the other two nodded.

"Yeah,'' Florence added, "I figure there'll be a lot of women there. Maybe I can find one for Mac.''

"And Tuck,'' Ruth added, sounding more eager than before.

"That will change the meaning of going shopping, won't it?'' Edith said with a giggle.

"Yes, it will,'' Ruth agreed. "But you know, since you and Mabel haven't produced any grandbabies yet, our bet's still on. I've never been a quitter and it won't happen now.''

"Me, neither,'' Florence assured her friends. There was a gleam in her eyes that had them all worried. What was she up to?

At Karl Delaney's tux shop you get more than a bow tie and cummerbund, you get free advice on your love life. As Karl says, "You don't own a tux shop for forty years and not know a little something about romance."

Join friends Dylan, Jack and J.T. as they pick up their tuxes and find surprise messages in their pockets.

SUDDENLY A DADDY
Mindy Neff April 1999

THE LAST TWO BACHELORS
Linda Randall Wisdom May 1999

COWBOY IN A TUX
Mary Anne Wilson June 1999

DELANEY'S GROOMS—Tuxedo rentals and sales—
matchmaking included!

Available at your favorite retail outlet.

HEART OF THE WEST

Where Every Man Has His Price!

Watch for Harlequin's top authors in this brand-new 12-book series!

Use this coupon and get $1 off the purchase of any
Heart of the West title.

You won't want to miss out.

Available at your favorite retail outlet in July 1999.

Look us up on-line at: http://www.romance.net   PHHOWCAN

HEART OF THE WEST

Where Every Man Has His Price!

Watch for Harlequin's top authors in this brand-new 12-book series!

Use this coupon and get $1 off the purchase of any
Heart of the West title.

You won't want to miss out.

Available at your favorite retail outlet in July 1999.

$1 off!

the purchase of any Harlequin®
Heart of the West titles.

Printed in Canada 6/99

Retailer: Harlequin Enterprises Ltd. will pay the face value of this coupon plus 8¢ if submitted by the customer for this specified product only. Any other use constitutes fraud. Coupon is nonassignable, void if taxed, prohibited or restricted by law. Consumer must pay any government taxes. Valid in U.S. only. Nielson Clearing House customers—mail to: Harlequin Enterprises Ltd., P.O. Box 880478, El Paso, TX 88588-0478, U.S.A.
Non NCH retailer—for reimbursement submit coupons and proof of sales directly to: Harlequin Enterprises Ltd., Retail Sales Dept., 225 Duncan Mill Rd., Don Mills (Toronto), Ontario M3B 3K9, Canada

PHHOWUS

Makes any time special ™

**Coupon expires
December 31, 1999.
Valid at retail outlets
in U.S. only.**

5 65373 00076 2   (8100) 1 05892

HARLEQUIN®

A M E R I C A N ◆ R O M A N C E®

®

COMING NEXT MONTH

#781 DADDY UNKNOWN by Judy Christenberry
4 Tots for 4 Texans
Tuck was thrilled to see Alexandra Logan back in Cactus, Texas—until
she told him she had a little problem. She was four months pregnant—
and, thanks to a slight amnesia problem, she didn't know who was the
man responsible!

#782 LIZZIE'S LAST-CHANCE FIANCÉ by Julie Kistler
The Wedding Party
Bridesmaid Lizzie Muldoon had resolved to attend the society wedding
stag, but somehow ended up with a *fake* fiancé! Groomsman Joe Bellamy
was the lucky guy for Lizzie. And she couldn't convince anyone he was
not her future husband—including herself....

#783 INSTANT DADDY by Emily Dalton
A whirlwind romance with a stranger resulted in the best part of
Cassie Montgomery's life—her son, Tyler. She never expected to see her
mystery man's picture in a magazine—advertising for a wife! Breathless,
Cassie replied. Would Adam Baranoff remember her—and welcome her
gift of instant fatherhood?

#784 AND BABIES MAKE TEN by Lisa Bingham
New Arrivals
A trip to the sperm bank and suddenly Casey Fairchild found herself
leaving the fast track behind and taking a job in a tiny Midwest town.
But life was anything but dull when her boss turned out to be a sexy
stud—and the father of quintuplets!

Look us up on-line at: http://www.romance.net

HARLEQUIN CELEBRATES

FIVE DECADES OF ROMANCE

In July 1999 Harlequin Superromance®
brings you *The Lyon Legacy*—a
brand-new 3-in-1 book from popular
authors Peg Sutherland, Roz Denny Fox
& Ruth Jean Dale

3 stories for the price of 1!

Join us as we celebrate
Harlequin's 50th Anniversary!

Look for these other
Harlequin Superromance®
titles wherever books are sold July 1999:

A COP'S GOOD NAME (#846)
by Linda Markowiak
THE MAN FROM HIGH MOUNTAIN (#848)
by Kay David
HER OWN RANGER (#849)
by Anne Marie Duquette
SAFE HAVEN (#850)
by Evelyn A. Crowe
JESSIE'S FATHER (#851)
by C. J. Carmichael